Behind Eclaire's Doors

Behind Eclaire's Doors

Sophie Dunbar

ST. MARTIN'S PRESS NEW YORK

Design by Diane Stevenson / S N A P ● *H A U S   G R A P H I C S*

Library of Congress Cataloging-in-Publication Data

Dunbar, Sophie.
    Behind Eclaire's doors / Sophie Dunbar.
        p. cm.
    ISBN 0-312-09280-6
      1. Women detectives—Louisiana—New Orleans—Fiction.
    2. Beauty operators—Louisiana—New Orleans—Fiction. 3. New
Orleans (La.)—Fiction. I. Title.
PS3554.U46337B44   1993
813'.54—dc20   93-10339
                                                          CIP

First Edition: July 1993

10 9 8 7 6 5 4 3 2 1

Dedicated to my husband,
the Trupins,
and the women of W.I.S.E., especially Susan and Anne.

The author wishes to gratefully acknowledge the enthusiastic instruction of Detective Sergeant Marlon Defillo of the Public Affairs Division, New Orleans Police Department, in the hope that he will understand and forgive the fears and failures of his fictitious counterparts, who will redeem themselves in future chronicles.

And to the staff of the wonderful Pontchartrain Hotel, special thanks for the use of the Bayou Bar, a luxurious suite, the Grand Court, and the penthouse!

Behind Eclaire's Doors

Chapter

1

It was 3:30 A.M., at the tail end of a sultry New Orleans July, but I got cold chills when I looked over the banister and saw what was lying on the floor below. Once before I had caught Dan with another woman. That's why he was my ex-husband. But the first lady had been very much alive, while this one definitely was not. And that night, he hadn't been wearing a bloodstained suit, like now. In fact, he hadn't been wearing anything at all. In one moment of time, the past fourteen months seemed to flash by like a film rerun at warp speed, a steamy melodrama starring yours truly and the man now crouched by a dead woman's body. Rated R.

Chapter

2

$\mathcal{W}$hen I was twenty-eight and still unmarried, *Tante* Jeanette Jennerette warned me, "Listen, *chér*. Won't be much left after you bury me, and your *oncle* done promised this here house to your cousin Eugene, him being the oldest. Got to find yourself a *mari* with three fat pockets, eh, *petite*?" Here, she would wink slyly and pat her right hip, then her left, then her crotch. "Two for the money and one for the love, *chér!*"

I could certainly agree with her point about the money. At the time, though I was enjoying some success as a hairstylist in a big salon, I also found it necessary to supplement my income by moonlighting, selling cosmetics in a ritzy department store.

However, when it came to the love part, my encounters had been few and unrewarding, and frankly, I had never yet experienced any sensation that I was willing to maybe end up dying for, given the state of the world these days.

It was purely coincidental that the only man on earth who ever rang my bell should turn out to be a fortyish frat daddy named Dan Louis Claiborne, who was most assuredly—and quite remarkably—endowed with those "three fat pockets" so dear to *Tante* J's heart!

Dan was from old New Orleans money, a senior partner in Blanchard, Smithson, Callant and Claiborne, one of the city's biggest, most important law firms.

Dan Claiborne had spent his entire life uptown. He didn't even have to move out of the family's State Street mansion to graduate from Tulane Law School, and St. Charles Avenue Presbyterian Church, scene of his first marriage to debutante and Newcomb grad Melissa Bonnie Bellamy (now remarried to the ex-husband of her maid of honor), was less than five minutes from home in the opposite direction.

I, Evangeline Claire Jennerette, on the other hand, had been brought up in the Bayou St. John area (*The Big Easy* territory), the orphaned child of a Danish au pair and a Cajun fisherman. My mother had loved to go out shrimping with my father, and they were killed when their boat went down during a storm somewhere in the Gulf of Mexico.

Oncle Hebert had been much older than his little brother, so his and *Tante* Jeanette's children were mostly grown when they took me in as a baby. He died when I was about seven, and it had practically always been just *Tante* J and me, except during the holidays when all the cousins and their kids converged onto the big, white wooden house on the water.

That's not to say I sling on an accordion and break into Cajun songs at the drop of a *chapeau*. I loved my family and heritage, and they returned the affection, but had always regarded me as something of a changeling.

Though I was proficient in the *patois*, my English lacked the spicy accent and bouncy cadence of the others. In looks, I had taken after my slender, golden-haired, creamy-skinned mother, and my taste in clothing ran more to tailored elegance than to the somewhat flamboyant outfits selected by my female relatives to show off their dramatic brunette coloring.

Conversely, to the Garden District crowd, I was merely a rather upscale swamprat, without even a university education to enhance my social status. Beauty college, apparently, didn't count, except *against*, even if it was the famous Marcel's Institute de Beaute.

Marcel Barrineau, the creative force behind a faculty composed of temperamental Europeans who consider themselves to be on the cutting edge, so to speak, of beauty technology, was descended from one of the original French families who had settled New Orleans and helped build Napoleon House, in preparation to receive their exiled emperor, who never arrived.

Marcel, with his aristocratic blood, and wealth, both inherited and acquired, was firmly entrenched in New Orleans society. Twice divorced and in his early fifties, he looked much younger, with a tall athletic frame, exquisitely groomed silver hair, and olive complexion. He also had this oddly pedantic speech pattern, which gave the entirely erroneous impression that English had not been his first language. It was, in fact, quite a charming little trick.

Every student who stayed on to work in one of the four Salons de Marcel, located throughout greater New Orleans, received a personal makeover.

"You are to be the cool blonde with a heart of fire," he'd decreed during our session, squinting at me in a visionary way. "And for this, we must snip a bit here and there from that picturesque but unmanageable name of yours. With your permission, I shall call you by the more sophisticated Claire Jenner."

As usual, Marcel was right. His version of my name fit me perfectly. So did his description.

When I graduated, Marcel handpicked me as his personal assistant, and, once I made him understand that my assistance did not extend into the boudoir, we got along fine.

Gradually, I built up my own following, and since I also

worked in a department store, my life was certainly full, but definitely unfulfilled, when I met Dan.

That night in late March, I was demonstrating a men's fragrance when a couple of guys in three-piece pinstripe suits sauntered up.

For some reason, certain clients expect all beauty service people to pinch hit for bartenders as confidants and confessors when necessary, so I was on the receiving end in both my day job and my night job. Consequently, I knew far more about one of the men, dumpy little Eustis Keller, than I wanted to, since he often used the store as a shortcut to his office building's parking garage on Baronne Street after hoisting a few in the French Quarter. By then, he would be generally loaded enough to feel in a buying mood, which quickly degenerated into verbose self-pity.

That's how I learned he was a junior partner in Blanchard, Smithson, Callant and Claiborne, working in the area of patent law and trademark/copyright infringement. He was frustrated that he only got to handle routine domestic cases, because the head of his department reserved all the glamorous international plums for himself, flying first class to Europe, taking meetings with the Sûreté, Scotland Yard, and Interpol. He, Eustis, hardly ever got to go exciting places, except for a few recent trips to France when the other guy was too busy.

According to Eustis, Blanchard, Smithson was damn lucky to have him. After all, he'd started out studying to be a research chemist or something before reversals in the family fortune forced him into Tulane Law School. Blanchard, Smithson had no right to pass him over for senior partner three times in a row, especially since he had graduated in the same class as the man who was now his boss. Well, someday he'd show them.

On and on Eustis would go, and while I rang up his extravagant purchases (Gucci Nobile for him, Molinard de Molinard for his wife, Obsession for the latest girlfriend) I felt both repulsed by and sorry for him.

Since my clients at Marcel's also talked a lot, I knew the other half of this story as well. Eustis's family tragedy occurred when his stockbroker father, having been alerted that his accounts were about to be federally audited, shot himself in the head, and that branch of Kellers was left nearly penniless. Eustis had to drop out of Johns Hopkins, to be sure, but, thanks to influential connections, he was able to attend Tulane Law School, all expenses paid, including frills like a car and a good fraternity.

Later he'd married Wilding Groves, an eerily beautiful heiress, who was heavily into riding and various blood sports, and Eustis seemed to have done pretty well for himself, all things considered. Frankly, I had a hard time working up much sympathy for his tales of woe, especially because Wilding was a client of Marcel's and, strange as she was, I liked her a whole lot better than I liked Eustis.

When Eustis spotted me, he introduced the man with him as Dan Claiborne, and I realized this was the guy he resented so much. Well, I could certainly see why. Poor Eustis was playing way out of his league. Dan Claiborne had not only a natural air of authority, but the physical presence to back it up: broad shoulders, burly chest, and dark, slicked-back hair. The face, with a full, sensual mouth and deep blue eyes under thick, dark brows, retained a mischievous boyishness, along with an unmistakable shrewdness.

"Danbo," Eustis chuckled, wafting Jack Daniels fumes into the cologne-laden air, "this is Claire Jenner. Cute lil' thing to be part coonass, isn't she!"

Dan pointedly ignored him. "Are you indeed of the

Cajun persuasion, Miss Jenner?" His voice, rich and husky, went straight to someplace deep inside me where nobody had ever been before, and those blue eyes caught and held mine tightly.

Instantly, my attention was completely absorbed by the man towering above me, and the effect was dizzying. I suddenly found it difficult to breathe, and my heart started beating an erotic rhumba on my eardrums.

A needles-and-pins sensation had me tingling from head to toe, but I retorted, as coolly as I could, "More accurately, half crawfish pie and half Danish pastry, Mr. Claiborne."

His eyes wandered down to my lips. "Now that," he drawled, "sounds like a most tantalizing combination. And while we're on the subject, may I have the pleasure of your company for dinner tomorrow night?"

Later Dan told me it was all he could do to restrain himself from grabbing me and applying his tongue to my tonsils, right then and there. I myself was seized with the overwhelming desire to unbutton his shirt, just to see if that chest was as big and hairy as it looked. (It was.) Although I did manage (then) to control the impulse, what did happen was that my hand gave an involuntary, but wildly suggestive, squeeze to the bulb of the atomizer I was holding, spritzing him liberally with Hugo Boss cologne. Naturally, he bought some. What man wouldn't?

We got married in a burning fever less than a month after our first date, and it was me-oh, my-oh, morning noon and night-oh! Of course, we realized that the mercury was bound to drop eventually; the human body can stand just so much of anything.

But we could never have guessed how quickly our marriage would crumble, or that murder had already been set in motion.

Chapter

3

*M*r. and Mrs. Claiborne were surprisingly cordial, considering that Dan sprung me on them without warning as their new daughter-in-law, after our tiny civil ceremony in a judge's chambers.

Traditionally, all firstborn Claiborne males have the initials D.L. The D can stand for anything, but the L must stand for Louis. In Dan's father's case, the D was for Dave, not David. Just as Dan was not an abbreviation of Daniel.

Dave Louis was burly like his son, but not quite as tall, with a full head of thick, white hair and those same blue eyes under still-dark brows. The eyes twinkled at me appreciatively.

Rae Ellen, Dan's lean, elegant, John Jay Salon blonde mother, was more reserved, possibly because it would fall to her to navigate the treacherous social waters with the news of her son's second marriage in less than a decade.

It was, perhaps, just as well that we were immediately leaving on a combined honeymoon/business trip to Paris, where Dan had been called to handle a sudden emergency for his biggest client, Poire Gillaud.

Poire Gillaud was militantly protective of its signature trademark, a golden pear, which appeared in some form on everything it made, from jewelry to luggage. Only Cartier was equal to commandeering the type of search-and-destroy missions that Gillaud launched on counterfeiters of its designs.

In fact, the wide gold band with a whopping four-carat, pear-shaped canary diamond Dan had slid onto my finger after the ceremony had been a wedding gift from Gillaud, in gratitude for the hundreds of thousands of dollars he'd saved them by busting a Puerto Rican sweatshop that was cranking out cheap versions of their famous *Poire et Grappe* silk fringed table and bed linens.

Paris with Dan was a dream. Not only was he unstinting with the plentitude of his middle pocket, he was extremely generous with what was in the other two as well! We shopped at many of the famous design houses, where he got special deals because he'd done work for most of them in the past.

But by far, the choicest items were from Poire Gillaud. Its clothing, shoes, accessories, jewels, and cosmetics were wonderful. And it had all begun back in 1895 with one fabulous fragrance concocted by Annette Gillaud. La Poire.

La Poire was as golden-green, as sweet and tart, as mellow and crisp as its name, and it was the most inimitable, expensive fragrance on earth. Not even Neiman Marcus ordered more than a few bottles at one time, opting for Gillaud's more modern lines, which were pricy enough.

Although Mr. Bertrand Gillaud, one of the two brothers who controlled the firm, took time to personally escort me on a tour through Poire Gillaud, I got the distinct impression he was preoccupied and nervous about his meeting with Dan. Afterward, he gallantly presented me with a special Lalique crystal pear-shaped flacon of La Poire, capped with a pavé diamond stem and leaves.

That night in our hotel suite, Dan and I consumed a large quantity of champagne and experimented with the erotic effects of La Poire upon various areas of the anatomy. As *Tante* Jeanette might have said, *"Le bon fais do do, chér,* yes!"

The next morning, Dan confided why he had been summoned to Poire Gillaud at this specific time. The unthinkable had happened! Someone had stolen half the formula for La Poire, which had been divided and secreted in two separate locations for safety. If a counterfeiter was able to develop a reasonable facsimile, it would be devastating for Gillaud.

As Dan explained, copyright, trademark, and patent violations are, in many ways, a form of art fraud. A fake Rolex is one thing. But how do you protect something as intangible as a fragrance that those who were able have been willing for nearly a century to pay big money to wear? Even in today's economy, there were still plenty of conspicuous consumers. No wonder poor Mr. Bertrand had seemed so upset yesterday.

Nevertheless, Poire Gillaud expected Dan to manage the recovery somehow, no matter that the thief could be anywhere in the world by now. At least, it would take whoever it was several months to brew up a usable batch, unless— heaven forbid—they managed to get hold of the other half of the formula. But for the moment all Dan could do was tighten security at Gillaud, activate his network, and follow his instincts. And his nose.

Then, so many bad things happened that I frankly had very little interest in whether the purity of La Poire remained unsullied or not.

Chapter
4

*I*n September, not quite five months after I became the second Mrs. Dan Louis Claiborne and set up housekeeping, including silver service for twelve in the Chrysanthemum pattern, in a small mansion on Octavia Street, *Tante* Jeanette, apparently feeling she'd done her best for me, died peacefully in her sleep.

During the spring and summer, Dan and I had been caught up in a mad whirl of attending and giving cocktail parties, dinner parties, brunches, and other entertainments, which constituted my official introduction to New Orleans Society. Despite my extremely humble origins, they were forced to tolerate me because I was married to a Claiborne.

But with the onset of autumn, in addition to my grief for *Tante* J, I found myself at loose ends. I wasn't used to having so much time on my hands, and while finally being admitted to the Junior League may be a pinnacle for some, it was not for me.

Also, our fever had subsided to a more normal temperature, and Dan and I were beginning to find out that we hardly knew each other at all.

One thing in particular I hadn't been aware of was Dan's football mania. Not only did we subscribe to a sports cable channel that promised we would not miss one thrilling moment of any college or pro playoff, in the entire U.S. and parts of Canada, our satellite dish was powerful enough to beam all the action of every animal, vegetable, and mineral Bowl, however obscure, right into our living room.

But it didn't stop there. Dan and some of his old fraternity buddies from Tulane were determined to relive their Green Wave glory days by recruiting a winning football team for their alma mater. These cronies still called each other by their old college nicknames. Dan was, of course, "Danbo." Eustis responded, appropriately enough, to "Tick." There were also "Trout," "Oak," "Pickle," and "Hat." Their mission was to cover every high school game being played within a seventy-five-mile radius, then meet to compare notes and begin campaigns to woo the favorites (within the ever-narrowing NCAA guidelines) to Tulane.

From then on, Dan began to withdraw from me, and I was seeing practically nothing of him. When he wasn't having late meetings at the law firm, or out of the country on business, or courting some high school quarterback, he said he was working at Tulane's Recruiting Office. That much was the truth, anyway. He just neglected to specify what, or rather whom, he was working on.

I found out the hard way, at a Tulane Booster Club party held at the Keller home in mid-November.

Marcel Barrineau, as a friend of the family, had been invited, and I spent much of the time chatting with him and Shelly, his latest "assistant." Marcel was trying to lure me back to work in one of his shops. "Many people keep inquiring for you, Claire," he told me persuasively.

Listening to Marcel, I realized that going back to work might be just what I needed to take my mind off whatever was happening to Dan and me, and agreed to give his proposition serious consideration.

I left them and got a fresh Bloody Mary from the bartender, carrying it over to the baby grand piano, where Wilding Keller, dressed in dull orange silk that set off her bronze hair, was running slim, nervous fingers over the keyboard and gazing blankly into the boisterous crowd milling through her home.

The French doors stood open, admitting a breeze that caused the fireplace to smoke slightly, and mingle with the smoke curling from the Balkan Sobranie cigarette dangling between Wilding's full, pale lips. Flames from banks of tall candles massed in silver holders, flickering across her exquisitely boned face.

Most people steered clear of Wilding, but, from the time I first met her as a client of Marcel's, I was intrigued by her solitary etherealness. I soon discovered that, from her space station, Wilding missed nothing, and was very well aware of Eustis's pathetic little escapades, which he thought he was so cleverly getting away with.

Now she slid down the bench to make room for me, while continuing to play weirdly assorted fragments of Gershwin, Cole Porter, Chopin, and some dark bits of what sounded like the *Theme from Dracula,* the really chilling one starring Frank Langella.

Suddenly, Wilding fastened her large, grey eyes on a laughing, tousled blond Valkyric surrounded by panting males, Eustis and Dan among them. "That," she informed me, flaring patrician nostrils toward the group in distaste, "is one of the secretaries in the coaches' office."

With a sickening little lurch of my heart, I saw that Dan was flushed with that rowdy, just-enough-booze-to-perform-fantastic look that had always been for me alone, up until such a short time ago. What had gone wrong?

But he hadn't even seemed to notice how good I looked that night. It was the first chance I'd had to wear my pink suit of tissue-thin wool, trimmed with black braid, that Dan himself picked out for me. "Oh, yes ma'am," he'd growled, when the fitting lady paraded me out to the show-room. "That little number makes you look like a luscious dish of those tiny little French raspberries. Remember what I said about them, Claire?" Indeed I did, and my knees went momentarily weak as I relived the occasion where he had demonstrated the amazing resemblance between two of those raspberries and . . . with horror, I realized I was close to tears.

I took a deep breath and repeated, "Secretary? No, Wild-ing honey. That's Frances James, the head cheerleader." I corrected her gently, trying not to glance down at her ump-teenth glass of rum/rocks/lime that was forming a white ring on the piano's beautiful ebony finish.

Poor Wilding! I was thinking. God only knows what she's getting at, when she abruptly stopped playing and slid one long, elegant arm around my shoulders, while with the other she raised her glass and drained the dregs, the ice rattling noisily against the antique lead crystal. Then she retrieved the cigarette she had left to smolder on the music rack and took a deep drag, heedless of the sparks that danced onto her lap. I pulled away slightly, trying to protect my suit, but Wilding gripped me harder.

"Yes, the head cheerleader," she breathed into my ear, engulfing me in a haze of smoke, rum, and Molinard de Moli-nard. "Exactly." Her luminous eyes impaled me. "She's very involved with recruiting." Wilding let go of me abruptly and stood up, swaying slightly. "*Very* involved," she repeated, investing the words with meaning, and drifted off.

She's very involved in recruiting. Wilding's sibilant utter-ance began to echo in my head, and nausea gripped me as I surveyed the room and confirmed that Frances and Dan were both missing.

That's when I decided to take a little moonlight stroll, only to be waylaid by Eustis Keller.

"Well, well! Claire!" he boomed jovially. His round, dissipated face was way too close to mine, resembling nothing so much as the "Tick" he answered to. His bourbon breath was making me even more queasy than ever.

"Haven't seen much of you lately!" he went on. "Listen, old Danbo sure is picking some winners these days. Take young Washington, for instance—"

I interrupted him. "No thanks, Eustis. You take him. I've seen and heard enough of young Washington to last me a lifetime. And now, if you'll excuse me . . ."

"Whoa, whoa!" Eustis grabbed my arm. "Where're you rushing off to?" He turned me to face him and wheedled, with porcine playfulness, "How 'bout sharing a little drinkie with old' Eustis the Cutesest?"

Despite my churning emotions, I realized the only way I could escape his clutches was to humor him.

"Why, thank you, Eustis!" I cooed. "But if I don't get upstairs to the little girls' room right now, I shall embarrass us both all over your lovely Sarouk!" I patted his pudgy cheek, barely managing to resist a powerful urge to claw it to ribbons. "Later, Eustis," I lied.

Aware of his eyes following me, I went halfway up the stairs. When, reassured, Eustis had turned his attention elsewhere, I was down and out through the French doors opening onto the terrace in a flash.

Despite the fresh air, my nausea increased, and I became aware of painful cramps in my lower abdomen. Oh, God, I prayed. Please don't let me start my period right now on top of everything else!

Somewhere in the back of my mind, a warning clanged. Not that long ago, when things had been good, they were so good that neither Dan nor I had bothered much with precautions. I had been so distracted by the sudden downhill slide our marriage seemed to be taking that, for the first time in my life, I was already several weeks late and hadn't even noticed.

I had no idea where I was going. It was blind instinct that carried me up an aisle of gnarled old oaks draped with Spanish moss that led to the garden.

The Keller property, facing Audubon Park, was practically an estate, inherited from Wilding's parents when they were both killed in a plane crash. Wilding regularly descended from her cloud to issue clear, crisp orders to a battalion of gardeners and groundskeepers. This insured that the hedges, flowers, and authentic Greek statues lining each side of the gravel path leading to a gazebo at the far end of an enormous pool would be maintained as impeccably as they had always been. And yet, there always seemed to be a faint whiff of decay hovering about the place.

There was a full moon that night, and it cast a pearly glow upon the pool, the gazebo, and the statues. Upon one female statue in particular, which seemed to have suffered none of the indignities of lost limbs or various vital appendages that had befallen the others. If anything, she appeared to be remarkably well endowed.

I froze in my tracks as from out of the oleander bushes appeared a big, naked man, his body burnished with luxuriant dark hair. He began to fondle the statue, and then I realized it wasn't a statue at all, but a completely bare-assed Frances James. And the man was my husband.

It was like being trapped in one of those hideous dreams where you are literally paralyzed, forced to face the terror that has been pursuing you all along. My head started spinning, and the nausea I'd been fighting finally overpowered me, and I threw up. Noisily.

Dan certainly hadn't realized it was his wife at the time. Thinking only that somebody had overindulged and was un- burdening himself too close for comfort, he and Frances si- lently melted into the shadows.

Chapter

5

*M*aybe it's nature's way of cushioning the shock, but it's amazing what totally bizarre thoughts can distract you while you are thrashing desperately in the iron jaws of your life's greatest tragedy. Even as I fell to the ground, I was concerned about getting runs in my stockings, and when I threw up, tried to make sure nothing splashed onto my beloved pink suit.

Kneeling next to a variegated camellia bush, gasping for breath between sobs and retches, I could no longer deceive myself that I had married Dan for nothing but lust and money. I was truly, madly, and totally in love with him.

God, I felt so awful! Even though the vomiting had stopped, my head pounded like it was going to split wide open, and the cramps were getting worse. I stayed on my hands and knees for a few more minutes, in sort of a daze. Maybe I was praying, but I honestly don't know.

Finally I was able to stand up. Mercifully, the rest of that terrible night passed in a series of blurs.

Stumbling clumsily back to the house . . . making my way, somehow invisibly, to the maid's bathroom off the kitchen . . . a ghostly face in the mirror with eyes like huge, dark cigarette burns . . . moving at a zombie pace into the living room . . . automatically accepting a glass of champagne from one of the Keller minions . . . Wilding, at the piano again, far away in her fog, but her big eyes opening wide at me in a flash of communication . . . the taxi ride home . . . huddled in Dan's old bathrobe for some shred of comfort, staring blindly at the television . . . Dan's return, blustering about why had I left . . . "I saw something that made me sick and I threw up, Dan" . . . his look of horrified comprehension . . . another wave of nausea . . . Dan holding my head . . . the sudden hemorrhaging . . . blackness.

I woke up about four o'clock the next afternoon to find myself in a private room at Touro Infirmary. Dan was sleeping in an armchair, head twisted uncomfortably to one side, wearing the same suit he had worn—and not worn—the night before.

They had left him to break it to me about the miscarriage, the lost baby that personified our life together that was gone, before we even knew we possessed it.

Dan, wretched and shaken, refused to leave me alone even long enough to get some coffee and smoke a cigar, which he badly needed. He admitted he'd been flirting and having drinks with Frances for several weeks. The strange thing was, he'd never intended to do anything more, and hadn't really wanted her at all. But when the new had worn off with us, he'd escaped into football, and there she'd been.

And there she'd been last night, after he'd uncharacteristically had too much to drink, and before he realized it, they were in the bushes. Ironically, that had been the only time anything had actually happened.

Just like me, he'd finally realized the potential for something incredibly deep between us, but it was too late to simply pick up and go on.

If we had any future together, we would have to start from scratch.

Chapter
6

"But, Claire! You can't possibly go to Haiti!" Mrs. Claiborne moaned. "The place is a tinderbox!"

Since Louisiana is still under the Napoleonic Code, there's no such thing as a quickie divorce in this state, unless it's for adultery, and that means a messy trial, the very kind of thing Gerard Gaspard, Esquire, is retained at high fees to prevent. Gerard, a plump, balding little eunuch, is the French laundry where New Orleans society sends its dirty linen.

In cases like ours, the wife usually withdraws gracefully to Reno, and, during the first numb, listless weeks following my miscarriage, when I had holed up with Dave Louis and Rae Ellen, I had passively agreed to follow tradition.

But suddenly I decided I wasn't going to go to Reno at all, but Haiti, where it only took forty-eight hours instead of six weeks. I just wanted to get it over with.

What's more, the only thing I wanted from Dan was enough money to buy that elegant little townhouse near Tulane University, because I planned to support myself by operating my own beauty salon from the first floor, and live upstairs. This was not some tacky condo, but an authentic townhouse that dated from the early 1900s, which had recently come onto the market after being lovingly restored to its original luster by a young professional couple, to finance their own divorce.

Since that would get Dan off the hook very cheaply, I was surprised when he proved so resistant to the idea. I didn't realize he already had other plans.

Rae Ellen gave up trying to talk me out of Haiti and looked helplessly at her husband.

Dave Louis put his big arm around me. "Are you sure this is what you want, honey?"

I fought back tears. "Yes," I whispered.

My father-in-law, who had taken early retirement from Blanchard, Smithson, due to a chronic kidney ailment, usually spent his days indulging in the gentle pleasures of golf and tormenting his stockbroker. But he evidently still managed to keep a hand in high places, since he simply picked up the phone and spoke directly to some big shot in the State Department, who assured him Haiti was between coups at the moment. And so, it was arranged.

The numbness had set in again, and I let myself be shuffled around like a deck of cards. From New Orleans to Miami and the lawyer's office, listlessly scrawling my name on papers I didn't bother to look at. They could've been a confession that I was Manuel Noriega's CIA mistress, for all I cared. From Miami to Port-au-Prince where the lawyer, Terry Kincaid, and I were met by a little bronze man named Racer.

Racer was Kincaid's island connection, one of an elite crew of natives who specialized in meeting people like me at the airport, then personally escorting us to each stop along the intricate bureaucratic route of establishing a forty-eight-hour residency, which entitled one to the dubious privilege of obtaining an instant divorce.

I hadn't really come back to life until that day (it was Valentine's Day) in a hot, crowded courtroom, where chickens roosted in the open windows. Crinkled old Judge Jacques had listened to my dull recitation of carefully rehearsed "testimony," then angrily slammed down his gavel, startling a squawk out of one of the hens and a restless flapping from another, declaring me divorced.

This made me break into hysterical sobs, protesting that I didn't really want a divorce.

"I have spoken!" he thundered angrily, banging the gavel again. "Now, Madame, remove yourself before I change my mind!" Kincaid jerked me out of the witness chair and hustled me from the courtroom.

Outside, the lawyer had mopped his face and snarled, "What the hell are you trying to pull, lady?" Turning on his heel, he left me standing on the dusty sidewalk.

On the drive back to the hotel, Racer explained my outburst had really upset Judge Jacques, who never relished his island being used as a divorce mill in the first place. He had personally waged an unsuccessful campaign to ban Steely Dan's hit "Haitian Divorce" from being played anywhere in the country.

He also resented the fact that American lawyers like Kincaid entered set pleas and collected lucrative fees that, for the most part, didn't stay in Haiti.

"But," Racer concluded with true Gallic pragmatism, much like *Tante* Jeanette's, *"Le Divorce*—it is one of our major industries!" He chortled. "Bigger than the rum, Madame!"

A few hours later, I received a terse phone call from Terry Kincaid at my posh Petionville Hotel, informing me that Racer would be picking me up at 6:15 to take me to the airport for a 7:00 P.M. flight back to Miami. But that mulish feeling came over me again, and I told Kincaid what he could do with that flight to Miami. I was going to stay in Haiti for a while, at least until after Mardi Gras. I felt more able to cope with a revolution than Mardi Gras. Kincaid didn't like it, but it was none of his business, anyway.

C h a p t e r

7

I certainly hadn't expected Dan to be waiting for me at the New Orleans airport, but there he was, eagerly scanning arrivals streaming off the Miami flight. As soon as I spotted him, my heart went into its usual bump and grind.

He appeared thinner, and a bit strained. I kind of missed that old Rip Torn just-fleshy-and-dissipated-enough-to-be-sexy look.

Silently he took my arm and guided me down to the baggage claim, then outside to where the law firm's Mercedes limousine was double-parked. Mmm, so he had brought out the big guns. As *Tante* Jeannette would've said, "A man don't bring a gun unless he's planning on shooting at something, no, *chér!*"

Rex, the firm's Creole driver, greeted me as cordially as if he were chauffeuring us to the opera while he held the door open, then discreetly raised the glass partition between us and himself before gliding out into traffic.

It seemed perfectly natural for Dan to put his arm around me, and just as natural for me to snuggle back into it like a favorite pillow, savoring his unique male scent, mingled with Boss cologne. "I thought we'd stop off at the Pontchartrain for a drink, maybe get a little dinner later," Dan suggested diffidently. "We need to talk, Claire."

Oh, that Southern Gent voice still turned me to jelly! I

briefly pressed my hand against his cheek, said yes, then turned away to watch as rain began to sprinkle the twilit highway.

The Pontchartrain Hotel on St. Charles Avenue is arguably the finest in New Orleans, having strictly maintained an elegant atmosphere of Europe's Golden Age throughout its venerable existence. Guests are still encouraged to leave their shoes outside the door at night, to find them freshly shined, sometimes even reheeled, in the morning.

For privacy, it was a perfect choice, because at this hour of the evening, most of the crowd we knew would be tanking up somewhere in the French Quarter. But, even if a few acquaintances did happen to stray in, the Pontchartrain's Bayou Bar was dimly lit. Dan chose a spot well in the back against the wall, under the Charles Reinike swamp mural, and the waiter quickly served us dry Negronis. More memories. That smoky little jazz bar in Montmartre . . .

All at once, Dan became very businesslike, opening his briefcase and extracting a blue folder, which he slid toward me.

I regarded it warily. "Well, I know it's something legal by that blue cover," I said. "But what?"

Dan, engaged in the complex ritual of lighting a big cigar, made sure it was burning satisfactorily before he replied. "I suppose," he drawled, taking a puff, "you could call it a little divorce present."

Gingerly I lifted the top sheet to see that it was the title deed, in my name only, to the townhouse! I was overwhelmed. Somehow, I seriously doubted Dan would go through with the purchase. Not so soon, anyway. And now that he had, the divorce seemed terribly final. Well, for God's sake, a divorce was pretty damn final, wasn't it? What was the matter with me?

I swallowed hard. "Uh—thank you, Dan. Very much," I mumbled. "I don't know what else—"

He waved me into silence and blew a sensual smoke ring. "It's not quite ready to move into yet, honey. There's a few details I need to find out from you. Like, which furniture and . . . wedding gifts, and whatever else you want from Octavia Street? Just get a list to me and I'll have it all delivered."

I was beyond speech. Everything was happening too fast. But wasn't this what I had asked for? And speaking of houses. Oddly enough, I hadn't even thought about where I was going to stay tonight!

As if reading my mind, Dan took two key rings from his pocket and placed them on the table. One I recognized as his set of Octavia Street house keys. The other held a Pontchartrain Hotel room key.

"I've rented a suite here," Dan said. "It's probably going to take a week or ten days to get everything squared away, so you can either just have my rooms, and I'll go back to Octavia Street, or vice versa."

Nervously, I took a much bigger swallow of my drink than I intended. The Negroni was having its usual aphrodisiac effect on me. Added to Dan's potent appeal, it was a combination nearly impossible to resist. The only thing that saved me was his matter-of-fact approach to the dreary, practical logistics of divorce.

I lowered my eyes again. "I—if it's all right with you, I'd prefer to stay here, at the hotel," I said. "I just don't think I could handle Octavia Street right now."

Without comment, his big hand closed over the house keys and returned them to his pocket.

Trying to match his nonchalance, I blurted, "Oh, I nearly forgot! Here's your copy of our divorce!"

I was surprised to see dismay on his face as he took the document I thrust at him and glanced over the two sheets of onionskin.

"Pretty flashy, isn't it?" he commented dryly, indicating the elaborate official seal, embellished with long, festive red ribbons.

"I have it on very good authority that '*Le Divorce*' is their biggest industry," I informed him loftily. "You can't blame them for getting a little artistic with it."

Dan grunted and caught the waiter's eye. Over another round of Negronis, he droned on with a laundry list of final details. I started to feel bored and irritated, and jet lag was rapidly rolling in. My eyelids drooped.

"So, Claire," he said finally. "Are you really still serious about opening your beauty shop downstairs?"

I roused to attention. During my absence, this was a subject I'd had plenty of time to think about.

"Oh, absolutely," I replied. "And, I've got the most perfect name for it."

Temporarily forgetting the somber occasion, I took another sip of my drink. "Listen, Dan. What do you think of this?" I paused for effect. "Eclaire."

His delighted laugh startled me. "Honey, I love it! Eclaire. What a great play on words, because it's you, exactly. Not only did you manage to pull in the E from Evangeline, but you are truly just a luscious little eclair yourself. Sweet and creamy on the inside!"

While I was still catching my breath, he became all business again. "Now. Did you plan to be on your own, or have another stylist, and a shampoo girl, or what? Talk to me."

I stared at him suspiciously, but he really sounded interested. "Well, to begin with, I'm definitely going solo," I told him. "I can always hire one of Marcel's students to help out with shampoos and errands when I get too busy. But I don't do nails. I will have to find a manicurist, eventually."

"Okay, then." Dan took out a pen and began to make notes on a cocktail napkin. "You need to let me have an estimate about how much all this is going to cost. It's not originally what I had in mind, but—I'm going to set you up in business, girl!"

By the third Negroni, we had arrived at the perfect concept for Eclaire, scrawled and sketched on a stack of Bayou Bar napkins. It would be luxurious and intimate. All equipment state of the art, but not one smudge of high-tech decor in sight. Instead, the design would be French Country. Terracotta tile floors, rough plaster walls washed in palest apricot; masses of fresh flowers every day; farmhouse pottery; Pierre Deux fabrics; pickled pine furniture; all necessary supplies hidden away in massive armoires.

"Like the one in our room at that darling inn in Provence with the featherbed and fireplace," I reminded him, then skidded to an abrupt verbal halt, realizing what I had said. That featherbed . . .

Dan's blue eyes kindled with memory and desire as he gently lifted my hand to his lips. He kissed the finger that still wore the big pear-shaped ring I couldn't bear to take off, in spite of everything, and said, "Yes, I know, baby. It seems like all roads lead back to us, don't they?

"I've been doing some deep thinking, Claire," he continued, caressing my hand between his. "You've been on my mind day and night. Especially night," he added meaningfully, causing my pulses to throb wildly.

"I know we covered a lot of this stuff before you left," Dan went on. "But I want you to hear me real good, right now."

He took a deep breath. "I must have been crazy, cheating on you, Claire. Until you came along, I don't know what the hell I thought love was supposed to be. But when I lost you, all of a sudden I knew that you were the only woman I have ever loved, the only woman in the world for me."

Squeezing my hand tightly, he kept right on talking, which was just as well, because I doubt if I could've uttered a coherent syllable. He was asking me to marry him again, only this time, we'd have a great big church wedding and start all over. In fact, we could even sell Octavia Street and move somewhere else, if I wanted to.

Then, embarrassed but determined to get it out, Dan confessed that he was so ashamed and rattled by the whole fiasco, he had gone to Oschner Clinic and gotten tested for AIDS and every other sexually transmitted disease there was a test for.

Dan concluded, "Better *believe* I intend to stay that way! Something happened to me through all this heartache, Claire. I finally understand what a total commitment actually means, and I'm ready to make one to you."

He took a last puff on his cigar and captured my hand again. "I want you to know I've been a very good boy, Claire." Dan's eyes narrowed at me. "But," he drawled, "it's been hard. It's been *very* hard." He pressed my hand between his thighs, and it was like touching a hot stove. "You see? But just for you, baby. I'm saving myself for you," he whispered hoarsely. Then he was pulling me along the seat until I was crushed in his arms, drowning in those deep, dark kisses I'd ached for, for so long.

At last, with a mighty effort, I pushed myself away, but he caught my wrist and said pleadingly, "Claire?"

The hotel room key was still lying on the table between us. I picked it up and managed to stand, although my legs were wobbling dangerously. I couldn't see him very clearly because my eyes were full of tears, but I spoke in his general direction.

"Dan, if you can swear to God you're telling me the truth, wait fifteen minutes and then . . . come upstairs."

I turned and fumbled my way blindly toward the elevators.

A quarter of an hour later, when he entered the room, I was showered and wrapped in his big bathrobe I'd found stretched across the bed, as if waiting to embrace me.

Then Dan Louis Claiborne did the most incredible thing. Kneeling in front of me, he buried his face in my stomach and began to sob. "Oh, Claire, I'm so sorry. I love you so much, baby. I swear to God!"

I slid to the floor and we held each other and wept together for a long, long time.

Chapter

8

"*L*ord have mercy!" Dan groaned as we lay tangled in a heap, drenched with perspiration. "I think I just had a heart attack!"

"Is that a hint for some CPR?" I inquired, and he pulled me down on top of him again.

We'd been making love for days behind the DO NOT DIS-TURB sign on our hotel room door. Dan had taken two weeks of vacation, and so far we hadn't seen or spoken to another living soul but Room Service.

The fever had struck again, hotter than ever, and though every inch of us was sore, bruised, and thoroughly ravished, it showed no signs of abating. Our only timeouts were to eat, rest, shower, or for Dan to shave when his beard got too rough for my tender skin. This was something far beyond the wildest sprees we'd ever been on together, totally consuming, and almost frightening.

At last, we were both so exhausted, we finally let the chambermaid in to bring some towels and change the sheets. Then we drank a good deal of strong coffee, and had a serious talk.

Down South, we've got these strange little bugs. I never knew their correct name, and I'm too much of a lady to refer to them by what they're commonly called. But all they do is copulate, even while trying to fly. Obviously, they can never maintain much of an altitude, or any sense of direction. They are constantly falling and bumbling, never getting anywhere, and generally looking like fools, but still copulating, by golly.

If we weren't careful, we were going to end up just like a couple of those stupid bugs. Like we had before, in fact. Completely burned out, with no other form of intercourse to fall back on. As Dan put it, there's only one kind of discussion you can have while you've got your tongues shoved down each other's throats. At some point, it was necessary to develop a dialogue that transcended "Ohbabybabycomeon-takeitrighttherelikethatharderfasterohmyGodthat'sgoodyes-yesyes!"

Since it was April, and we had decided on an August wedding, that gave us four months to invest the same amount of energy into each other's minds as we had into each other's everywhere else. No subject could be declared taboo, be it art, literature, food, politics, heaven, hell, or Jesus.

But the only way we could possibly do that was to go very cold turkey indeed. We had to swear off sleeping together until after the ceremony. Ground rules were simple and real-istic; anything and everything but *it*, to commence when I moved into the townhouse and Dan returned to a blameless bed on Octavia Street. The bonus to all this was, we would wind up having an actual Wedding Night, in a nineties kind of way!

Meanwhile, there were still a few more days until check-out time at the Pontchartrain . . .

Somewhere near the end, we became so fused together that it suddenly felt like we had literally switched bodies. "My God, Claire!" Dan observed. "If we ever get to where we can do this with our *minds*, we'll be downright dangerous!"

Chapter

9

$\mathscr{I}$t was the end of May, and at last, the burgundy, green, and gold-striped awning that ran from the front door down to the sidewalk was up. Eclaire was ready to cut loose, as it were.

There was going to be a cocktail reception the next evening, with a piano player, a luscious buffet, and for dessert, a full range of mini-eclairs. Marcel and my once-and-future-mother-in-law Rae Ellen had compiled a guest list, and between them, virtually every socially acceptable female, and a good number of males, with their own hair and somebody's money to spend on it, had been invited. Marcel had even sneaked in a few names of clients he wanted to lose. Judging from the RSVPs, we were expecting around five hundred people tomorrow night, including escorts.

I had been in a frenzy of activity for days, making sure that all the special little touches Dan and I planned were just right. It was his idea to have everything upholstered in the infamous *Poire et Grappe*. Naturally, Gillaud was delighted, and came through with such a good deal, we couldn't afford not to use the stuff.

At the same time, I was trying to get the upstairs livable without making too big a project of it, since I wouldn't be there that long. Dan was helping me as much as he could, and had just carried up a heavy box of things I'd asked for from Octavia Street, along with a six-pack of Oranjeboom beer. I watched as he twisted open a bottle and swallowed thirstily.

A ripped Tulane tank top stretched across his barrel chest, its mat of thick, dark hair glistening with sweat from his exertions. An extremely short pair of cutoff Levi's bared those disturbingly vast, furry thighs. As if drawn by a magnet, my eyes fastened on his fly, and Dan caught me looking. In two seconds, he had me pinned against the built-in refrigerator, covering my mouth with hard, beery kisses, grinding his hips into mine and giving me some bad news, all at the same time.

"Baby, don't get mad, but I'm sorry. I won't be able to be here tomorrow night," he informed me, while his tongue wound concentric circles around my right ear. "I just found out I've got to fly to Paris first thing in the morning."

"Oh, no! Dan! Not tomorrow!" I wailed, and did a few things with my own tongue for revenge, noting with pleasure that he almost hyperventilated.

"Shit!" he growled, when he could talk again. "You did that on purpose, and I will find a way to get even with you!"

Dan backed off and I turned to press my forehead against the Sub-Zero's smoothly humming stainless steel so I couldn't see him making the vital adjustments to his cutoffs. That wouldn't help the situation at all.

I was very upset at this glitch, because I had counted on a tuxedoed Dan being at my side tomorrow night, giving me the courage and confidence I needed to face this crowd in an entirely new capacity. I felt a surge of panic.

"Okay, babycakes," Dan chuckled. "You can turn around now."

Still, I kept my back to him until he took me by the shoulders and revolved me to face him.

"Come on now, Claire. Look at me," he commanded. "You've got to know, after all we've been through, I wouldn't just run out on you at a time like this. But I'm afraid there's bigtime *merde* getting ready to hit the fan at Gillaud.

"And another thing," he added. "Don't tell anybody, not even Mama, where I've gone. Especially don't tell Tick. You know how he gets."

As I met his blue eyes, the insidious worm of doubt receded. "I'm sorry, Dan," I sighed. "It's just, I'm not sure I can carry it off all by myself."

Dan stroked my cheek and smiled. "Then maybe it's best I won't be there, honey. See, it's real important to me that you understand I got behind all this"—his gesture encompassed the townhouse—"because I happen to believe in your talent.

"And listen, darlin'. Tomorrow night, when you're standing down there in the middle of that fabulous place (which I frankly *do* take a whole bunch of credit for), looking like a queen in that gorgeous emerald-green gown, with your golden hair piled on top of your head, you're going to have something special to remind you I'm right there with you."

Rummaging through the carton he'd brought upstairs, he extracted a large, flat, black velvet box and held it out teasingly in front of him.

"Is this the part in the movie where you open the lid, then snap it shut real fast?" I joked excitedly.

"Well, why don't you just waltz on over here and find out?" Dan invited.

Inside lay a stunning, simple, square-cut emerald pendant on a rose gold figaro chain and matching stud earrings.

"Oh, Dan!" I breathed, as he took it from the box.

"Should go perfect with the dress, don't you think so? And just in case you're wondering, this was no freebie from a grateful client, let me tell you!"

He fastened the pendant around my neck, then traced it down with his lips. "Uh-huh," Dan murmured. "I thought it would fall right about . . . there."

C h a p t e r

10

*B*y nine the next evening, Eclaire was packed with a well-heeled crowd that swarmed over the buffet of Louisiana caviar (red beans and rice, to the uninitiated), hot sausage, and fried oyster po-boys like they didn't know where their next meal was coming from.

The satisfied buzz of a full-blown feeding frenzy was punctuated with ripples of live piano music and the solid *thunk* of ice cubes against glass. Dan had been fortunate enough to secure the services of one Mr. Gus, a bartender famed for his skill with Sazerac cocktails, Bellinis, and of course, Negronis.

At last, I was able to breathe a sigh of relief. The response had been better than I could have possibly imagined. From the moment my guests crossed the threshold, they were captivated, oohing and ahhing at everything.

A photographer from the *Times-Picayune* wanted to photograph the large framed oil portraits of women and men with fabulous hair that lined the walls, instead of the usual blown-up androgynous head posters. I had commissioned Ambrose Xavier, a Jackson Square street artist, to supply me with a new series each quarter. If the newspaper featured his paintings, it could mean a big break for him. I gave the T-P man my permission to shoot, on the condition that he include the artist as well, and left the handsome Creole posing happily alongside his work.

We had used some actual photos to demonstrate my hairstyles, but they were a mix of 5 × 7's and 3 × 5's, framed in pewter, bronze, or gilt, subtly clustered in groups on tables and shelves like snapshots of family and friends.

In one corner, an enormous crystal vase, holding the three dozen Brandy roses Dan had sent, stood on a tall pedestal.

Now, just for fun, I glanced at the large appointment book, covered in *Poire et Grappe*, naturally, which had been left lying discreetly untended on the reception desk, the ribbon marking my official opening date, June 1. With delight, I discovered that I was already booked solid for the entire month, and a few names had spilled over into July!

I decided this called for a celebration, and made my way to the bar, receiving compliments and congratulations along the way in a kind of daze.

Mr. Gus mixed me a dry Negroni, which I sipped with caution. My stomach had been so full of butterflies, I hadn't been able to eat all day long.

"Honey, if I wasn't such a serious, dedicated investigative reporter, I'd be taping a piece on this bash for the eleven o'clock news!" drawled a voice behind me.

With pleasure, I turned to greet my best friend, Charlotte Dalton.

"Hey, Charlo!" I exclaimed as we hugged. "I'm so glad you're here! I wasn't sure you would make it in from D.C. in time!"

Charlotte gave a rich chuckle. "Sweetie, what's a bunch of loose-legged politicians compared to this fabulous event? They'll still be there next week, God help us! But in the meantime, now that you're back in business, Claire, I came to get me a good haircut!''

She flung out her shoulder-length chestnut mane with one hand in a mocking gesture and laughed again, causing her paper-white skin to shimmer and her green eyes to dance. Charlotte looked more beautiful than ever, in a pumpkin-colored grosgrain satin suit with puffed shoulders and big rhinestone buttons.

"Bring your drink and let's try to grab a few minutes to catch up, Charlo," I said, pulling her by the hand until we found a spot of privacy in one of the windowseats that looked out onto the garden.

Charlotte lapped at her Sazerac and gazed around her thoughtfully. "Well, I must say, little lady. You've really accomplished something original here! I've never seen anything quite like this before."

"Charlo, I didn't do it alone. There's a whole lot of Dan that's gone into this project," I informed her.

She snorted. "And from the rumors I hear, there's a whole lot *more* of Dan that's gone into *you*, honey! Ha! Don't you dare bother to deny it, Claire Claiborne! You're blushing right down to your considerable cleavage!"

Then Charlotte did a double take. "My word! What a magnificent emerald! And earrings to match! But what, no tiara? What do you have to do to get the tiara?"

As usual, Charlo and I were soon hooting with laughter. I just hoped, when she was my maid of honor, we didn't wind up rolling in the aisle, instead of gliding down it gracefully.

Finally she got serious. "I hesitate to ask this, Claire, but were is Dan tonight?"

I shrugged. "Sorry, I can't tell even you, Charlotte. Some sort of hush-hush work thing."

Charlotte crunched a piece of ice reflectively. "But, it *is* going to be Dan, isn't it, Claire?" she asked, oddly insistent. "You've got that big stallion permanently plugged in at the crotch, to put it genteelly?"

"Oh, Charlo! Now that is what I call finishing school genteel!" I laughed. "And if I say no, you'll just look smug and point to my blushing bosom again! So, what is this really all about, *chér?*"

She smiled weakly. "You think you're so smart, don't you? All right. It's about Joey Antoine. I just wanted to make sure . . ."

I was startled, to put it mildly. Sergeant Joseph Antoine, of the New Orleans Police Department, one gorgeous brunet hunk with a chip on his shoulder, was the last guy I'd dated before Dan, and it had always been a mystery to me why he'd kept asking me out, since there was never one iota of chemistry between us.

Joey was from the Ninth Ward, a nearly mythical political territory somewhere between the Garden District and the Mississippi River. The natives, mainly Irish and Italian, with some French and a few other things thrown in, are sometimes called "Y'aats," because the local greeting "Where y'aat?" originated with them. The place also seems to be a breeding ground for men who sound like Dr. John, and Joey was one of them, with a voice like dark roast coffee beans going through a grinder.

It was a total lie, but Joey had put out the story that I'd dumped him for Dan, because Dan was Uptown.

Even considering Charlotte's amazing knack for winding up with Mr. Wrong every time, this was really pushing it, especially given Joey's festering class resentment and Charlotte Dalton's yard-long Southern blueblood pedigree. It was a choice piece of irony that Joey was assigned to Homicide in the Second Division. Uptown.

But I tried to show some enthusiasm. "If you're worried that I mind, please forget it, Charlo!" I said, truthfully.

Charlotte cleared her throat. "I'm glad that's okay then. I didn't want to do anything awkward. Actually, I invited him as my escort tonight. He said he'd be here about ten o'clock." She consulted her Concord Delirium, keeping her eyes down.

Impulsively I leaned over and kissed her cheek. "Gonna tell you a secret, *chér*. Joey and I *never*."

Charlotte's head jerked up and her eyes widened. "You mean, never *ever?*"

"Listen!" I ordered. "Joey Antoine and I had about as much sizzle between us a couple of store window dummies!"

Charlotte hugged me. "Claire, I can't tell you how relieved I am to hear this!" She grinned. "I reckon that hung old bull just flat spoiled you for anybody else! Hey, I still have enough time to freshen up before Joey gets here!" And she scuttled off to the powder room.

A moment later Wilding Keller materialized next to me, with Eustis, for once, at her side.

"I signed your book, Claire," Wilding murmured, smiling foggily.

Wilding happened to be one of the clients Marcel wanted to discard, and I was glad to have her. "It will be an honor to work on your hair, Wilding." I said. "In fact, I've wanted to get my hands on that beautiful bronze stuff for ages!"

"What about me, Claire?" Eustis wheedled, his eyes on my emerald. At least, I hoped that's where they were. "Don't you want to get your hands on mine too?"

"Only," I retorted, "to pull it out by the roots, Eustis!" Maybe that was cruel, since he had transplants, but he deserved it. And anyway, I hadn't been referring to his hair.

Wilding made a sudden noise, and I realized she was laughing! I'd never heard her laugh before.

A flush of anger suffused Eustis's face, but before he could say anything, another woman joined our happy little group. Immediately Eustis forgot all about everything else. "Ah, there you are, Angie!" he greeted her, with a dopey grin.

Oh, no. I knew the signs. This was Eustis Keller's latest. I glanced hastily at Wilding, who stood poised and graceful, attention focused on something completely invisible to me.

Eustis introduced the newcomer as Angie Labiche (pronounced La-beesh) recently arrived from France. Angie was one of those dark, wiry, monkeyish Parisiennes who somehow manage to exude sexuality and make every other woman in the room feel like she's either too much, or not nearly enough.

She was older than the usual Eustis-type cutie, I guessed in her late thirties, and I had a bad feeling that this time, he'd bitten off a whole lot more than he could chew.

For her part, Angie wasted no time in sizing me up. Her sharp, black eyes avidly assessed everything, from my gown to the emeralds, as she initiated the traditional French handshake.

I had to offer my left hand, because I was clutching a damp, empty glass in my right, and when she got a load of the Poire Gillaud ring, I was frankly surprised to see it was still there when she let go.

My immediate impression of Angie Labiche was negative. I didn't like the way she looked at everything, from my salon to my jewelry, as if to say "I will take this if I want it!"

At least she spoke excellent English, so we were spared an excess of coy *moues* and sentences punctuated with " 'Ow you say?"

Eustis was prattling on importantly about how he'd managed to pull strings to get Angie a green card in record time, when Wilding tuned in long enough to remark abruptly,

"And Eustis also managed to find Miss Labiche a lovely place to stay, Claire. Our guesthouse!"

A cold anger filled my throat. "How . . . extremely *generous* of you, Eustis."

Turning to Angie, I added, "And now that you so miraculously have your green card, what do you propose to do with it?" Being a lady, I didn't offer my own suggestion.

Eustis put in, "Well, that's kind of where you may be able to help, Claire. In fact, I wanted to talk to Dan about this very thing."

He craned his pudgy neck and frowned. "Where is old Danbo, anyway, Claire? I haven't seen him all night."

I waved my hand nonchalantly. "Oh, wouldn't you know it? He suddenly had to go out of town on some boring old business crisis!"

Eustis grew very still. "What crisis? Where did he go? Did he go to Europe? When is he coming back?" Eustis rattled off the jealous questions toward me like a barrage of machine-gun fire.

I did my best to look vacant. "Gosh, Eustis! He's back and forth so much, I can't keep track. I was pretty upset that he wouldn't be here tonight, is all I call tell you."

"That's too bad," Eustis said perfunctorily. "Anyway, as I was fixing to mention, Angie here is a manicurist!"

Already I could see what was coming, but I merely waited, saying nothing.

Angie smiled wolfishly. "Eustis thought that your charming little salon might benefit from having a manicurist such as myself, who has held positions in the best places in Paris. Nina Ricci, Dior, Chanel . . ."

"The last place Angie worked before she came over here was Poire Gillaud!" Eustis blurted proudly.

Well, well. So that explained how she'd gotten her hooks into him.

I was thinking fast. As much as this poisonous French spider gave me the jimjams, it was also true that the names written in my appointment book were women who'd expect to be able to get a manicure if they wanted one. Since I was brand new, they'd be willing to make allowances on the first visit, but not the second.

Undeniably, there would be a definite cachet for Eclaire to boast a genuine French manicurist who could drop heavy names like Dior and Gillaud.

"Hmmm. Well, I'll have to discuss this with Dan first," I told Angie. "But maybe we could work something out. In the meantime, why don't I introduce you to Marcel Barrineau? I know he could use some freelance help."

"Ah, New Orleans!" Angie exclaimed, her dark eyes glittering mockingly. "Everyone is so kind!"

The minute I introduced Marcel and Angie, I realized they were birds of a feather.

Angie, as an experienced Frenchwoman, would no doubt provide Marcel with a stimulating new challenge that was lacking in all those "special assistants."

And Marcel, who had a reputation of being very generous for "favors received," could expect to be even more so, if Angie had anything to say about it! I could almost hear her calculator whirring as she totaled up his appearance, from silk tie to handsewn loafers.

I sometimes wondered just how Marcel managed to live and love on such an opulent scale. Sure, he made lots of money from his beauty institute and the various shops, but he also had a staff of highly paid operators, two ex-wives, and three children enrolled in *L'Ecole Française*.

Anyway, I thought with satisfaction, as I stood back and

watched them go to work on each other, this would spell big trouble for Eustis Keller!

I left them to it and started circulating among my guests again. The piano was playing a slow jazz version of "If Ever I Cease to Love."

Arms locked around each other, eyes closed, Joey Antoine and Charlotte Dalton were swaying to the music, and they were the only couple dancing. Just then Charlotte's lashes fluttered open, and she smiled at me over Joey's broad shoulder. I smiled back, but I still felt uneasy about them.

"Hi, darlin'." Dan spoke softly when I answered the phone hours later. "I hate to wake you up, but I just had to find out how things went."

"It was fabulous, except for your not being here. And those roses were absolutely perfect!"

When I had regaled him with some highlights of the evening, he said, "See there? Didn't I tell you you could carry it off? I'm proud of you, baby!"

I told him about Eustis and the Angie Labiche menace, and how disturbed I was with the way they'd put me on the spot about her coming to work at Eclaire, even though I acknowledged she could be a unique asset.

"By the way," I wound up, "I thought you'd like to know your pal Eustis sure did quiz me as to your whereabouts. And guess what else? Eustis met Angie when she was working in the salon at Poire Gillaud. How's that for a big old coincidence!"

Dan was silent for so long, I thought we'd lost the connection. "Well, now. That's very interesting," he said finally. "You know, Mam'selle Angie Labiche sounds like exactly the right manicurist for Eclaire. We'll see when I get back, okay?"

"Okay, darling," I murmured drowsily.

"Claire." Dan's voice roused me again. "I've got a few hours before I meet Bertrand for dinner, so I want to take a nice long nap. But I don't think I'm going to be able to sleep, because I'm lying here bare-assed in a kingsize bed, with a big old kingsize you-know-what."

I was certainly awake now. "And just what," I wondered aloud, "do you expect me to do about your predicament? After all, Dan, even you aren't quite kingsize enough to stretch all the way across the Atlantic."

Dan caught his breath sharply. "Don't be too sure about that!" he muttered. "Just suppose I managed it?"

I told him, in detail.

"You better watch out, woman!" Dan warned. "Because come August, I am going to lay you down someplace, and you will definitely *not* be getting up again for a considerable length of time!"

"Oh, yeah?" I taunted him a little breathlessly. "Big talk comes easy."

"Baby, that ain't the only thing!" Dan informed me.

Chapter

11

Things had not gone well in Paris. "*Merde* hit the fan?" I sympathized.

"Hit the fan and blew right back in my face!" Dan agreed irritably. "I don't know what I'm gonna do about it, either."

Glad for the distraction, he dove into our wedding plans with gusto, suggesting it might be a whole lot more fun to keep it a secret until the invitations were sent out in mid-July. The formal afternoon ceremony would be held at the Episcopal church Dan's parents attended on Josephine Street, and where we had put in an occasional guest appearance ourselves, followed by a blowout reception with two bands, Cajun and Dixieland, in the Grand Court of the Pontchartrain Hotel.

"When I spoke to the manager, he told me they retired our room number after we checked out!" Dan teased.

Meanwhile, Eclaire was getting to be a hot hair ticket, and I hired Renee Vermilion, one of Marcel's top students, as my assistant. Then Dan and I paid a visit to Angie, who was currently working at Salon de Marcel on Carrollton Avenue, to discuss her coming to Eclaire.

After one look at Dan, Angie had ignored me completely, and I didn't like that look. It was twin to the one she'd aimed at everything I owned the night of Eclaire's grand opening party, and she gave Dan full blast with both barrels.

That perfect English inexplicably acquired a more flirtatious French accent, and her conversation took on a charming hesitancy which seemed to require a lot of assistance and reassurance from Dan.

At the same time, she was speaking to me in the primordial language of Woman, which is the only true Esperanto and which requires no interpreter. "I want this man and I am going to get him."

I was ready to cancel the offer. Surely there were plenty of excellent manicurists available without inviting the fox into the henhouse. Also, I knew Marcel wouldn't be pleased, even though it had been understood that Angie would come to Eclaire when we were ready. He was very happy with the way their "arrangement" was working out. But Dan, for some reason, failed to pick up on my signals and hired her on the spot.

As we walked away, I could feel her triumphant smirk, quivering between my shoulder blades like a stiletto.

Anticipating my anger, Dan said, "Claire, I need you to go with me on this, and don't ask any questions, because I can't answer them."

"I thought no subject was taboo?" I reminded him.

"This one is," he said briefly, not meeting my eyes.

I had to admit, Angie certainly pulled her weight financially, pampering fingers and toes for exorbitant prices in what the original owners of the townhouse had intended to be the breakfast room. But she would also chatter away to her clientele, male and female, about how *très distingue* she thought Dan was, *un homme formidable*, and he was single, no?

Considering Dan's lousy track record, it wasn't long

before people started wondering if Dan Claiborne was up to his old tricks again. More than once, I found myself on the receiving end of pitying looks. "Caring friends" informed me Angie turned up nearly every evening at the French Quarter bar that was a big lawyers' hangout, where Dan was a habitué, and almost always managed to snag a seat next to him.

I certainly didn't understand why Dan was allowing this to go on, but he had insisted I trust him, and I was either going to or I wasn't, so I made myself ignore the whole thing.

Marcel, of course, was among the first to hear the jungle drum, and he looked upon it as a huge joke. Not only was he an old hand at the game, he knew all the players very well, indeed. Especially Angie.

Not so Eustis. When the gossip belatedly reached his ears, he started turning up at odd hours during the day, cornering Angie between appointments. After a while, Eustis would emerge, looking reassured, though I was willing to bet she hadn't slept with him since the night she met Marcel! The only reason I could imagine she continued to keep him on the string was because she was still living in the Keller guesthouse.

Wilding Keller just happened to be at Eclaire on one of these occasions. In an extraterrestrial kind of way, Wilding looked after her own interests. For example, she came in once a week for shampoo, conditioner, and blow dry, and made a point of having Angie do her nails every time. Angie hated this, because she knew Wilding was reminding her of who they both really were.

One day when Eustis barged in he saw Wilding sitting in my chair and nearly had a stroke.

"Hello, Eustis," Wilding greeted him politely.

At that moment, Angie stepped into the room, and took in the situation at a glance.

"Wuhh-wuhh-wuhh!" bleated Eustis, and beat a hasty retreat.

Angie withdrew to her lair in silent fury, and Wilding lowered heavy eyelids, smiling to herself as I snipped minute ends from the thick, bronzy hair.

"He's hardly ever home anymore." Wilding's voice drifted back to me over the drone of the blowdryer. "But he's not always with her either. I always look in the guesthouse windows to make sure," she added matter-of-factly.

"And sometimes, when he gets back, Claire, he smells . . . funny. It's not booze, though. More like . . . chemicals . . . only . . . I don't know . . . sweeter . . . fruit." Wilding trailed off somewhere I couldn't follow, which was too bad, since it was the crux of all the horror that followed.

One of the things Dan had discovered as we learned more about each other was that I was fascinated by angels. From somewhere the man had unearthed an antique angel door-knocker, which was perfect for Eclaire's front door. From there, the angel theme had expanded to include the logo, which was a precious little angel's head, with wings out-stretched over ECLAIRE spelled in tapestry letters.

Dan hadn't officially kept a key to the townhouse, because he wanted to demonstrate he respected my owner-ship. But sometimes, if he wanted to drop by late at night, he would use the spare we kept concealed in the angel doorknocker's hollow wings so I wouldn't have to come downstairs to let him in.

We thought it was the most romantic idea in the world, deliciously reminiscent of Cary Grant and Ingrid Bergman in

Indiscreet. Mistakenly, we thought this little arrangement was known only to us.

But, even after we learned otherwise, I was so used to keeping the key there, I just never got around to taking it out, until it was too late. The only thing that stopped me from blaming myself for what happened was that it would have happened anyway. Just not in my shop.

Although we were keeping mostly to ourselves these days, we did try spending a few evenings with Joey and Charlotte, but it didn't work out. Joey's resentment of Dan and everything he stood for always ended up putting a blight on things, which kept Charlotte constantly on edge, her natural spontaneous humor quenched.

Dan was amazingly tolerant when these episodes occurred, but Charlotte finally lost her temper on one occasion. "For God's sake, Joey!" she'd nearly shouted. "Get off it! We can't all be born on holy ground in the Ninth Ward, you know! Besides, I was a big old Atlanta debutante, and I went to Sweetbriar. What am I supposed to do? Crawl up stone steps on my knees, or something?"

I was getting very worried about Charlotte. Joey, like a vampire, was draining away her *joie de vivre*. But that night, in the ladies' room at Bayona, after Joey had managed to ruin a fabulous dinner, Charlotte waved away my commiserations.

"Thanks, Claire. But honey, we both know this ain't the first time I've jumped into the sack and found out I've landed in a bed of nails! And speaking of nails!" She put down her lipstick and searched my face in the mirror.

"What's all this I'm hearing about Dan and that Frenchified weasel of a fingernail jockey, Claire?" she demanded with her usual forthrightness.

I laughed nervously. "I . . . don't know what you mean, Charlo!"

"Oh, come on, Claire!" she flashed irritably. "This is me, remember? They have been seen out together, you know!" Charlotte tossed her head, and I admired how the shining chestnut strands swirled heavily around her face. I did give a good haircut.

"It's easy to see how Angie managed to get that porker Eustis over a barrel," she mused. "And Marcel is more than a match for her. But La Bitch would like everybody to think she's got something going with Dan, as well!"

Slanting a quick glance to gauge my reaction, she giggled. "Of course, none of your real friends believe a word of it. We've all seen what you do to that big old sperm whale the minute he gets around you. Honey, they can hear him bellowing and pawing the ground all the way to Bogalusa!"

Charlotte kept on in this vein, mixing animal metaphors until we were both doubled up laughing.

"When you guys were dancing the other night," she managed to gasp, "the poor man had to struggle so hard to keep the lid on his love machine, the whites of his eyes actually turned red! *Red,* I tell you! Remember the Incredible Hulk? Exactly what he looked like! It's a total miracle his pants just didn't go ahead and split wide open!"

By now my sides ached and tears were streaming down my cheeks. "Oooh, stop!" I begged. "You're making this up!"

"No, I swear!" Charlotte insisted. "And no man in his right mind is going to blow a burning love like that twice in one lifetime. Plus, Dan is a whole different person than he was eight months ago. And so, I repeat. What the hell is with this Angie business?"

I shrugged. "Charlo, that's something we don't discuss. But I think it's all tied in with Dan's work."

"Hmmm." Her green eyes sharpened speculatively. "I wonder if there's a story for a hardworking girl reporter in there somewhere? International intrigue, Cartier hiring hit men, maybe?"

I laughed. "I don't know, but if there is, I promise you an exclusive. But, whatever's going on, I believe I could trust Dan with my life, crazy as that may sound."

Charlotte nodded soberly. "Somehow, I believe you truly could. You and Dan are just meant to be. Am I right?" she added cunningly.

"Wait and see!" I teased. I'd have to tell her soon, though. August wasn't far away now.

Of course, I didn't know then how long it was going to take us to get through July, or how awful it was going to be, or that I actually would have to trust Dan with my life.

C h a p t e r

12

I have yet to spend a July Fourth in New Orleans when it didn't rain, and sure enough, this one had dawned muggy and sullen, even though yesterday had been fair, unseasonably mild, and bone dry.

As usual, by 2:00 P.M., the annual Blanchard, Smithson, Callant and Claiborne company barbecue, held on the grounds of Leighton Blanchard's River Road plantation, had moved indoors. When it did, by mutual consent, Dan and I kept right on moving, through the house and out the front door, sprinting through the downpour to the shelter of his big BMW.

We drove leisurely through the rain along the levee, playing the tape of the Cajun band we'd booked for our reception, a group called Bubba Smoke and the Swamp Society. Dan, who had a great voice, was singing along with his favorite cut, "La Bonne Femme Quelle Hot Stuff."

He slid his eyes over to me and said, "Depending on how much champagne I imbibe at our *fais do do,* I just might get up there and serenade you with that song, baby!"

"Where are we going?" I asked idly.

"Hmm. Well, we could go back to your place and open a bottle of that red wine I brought back from France last time. And maybe later on, you'll whip up one of those gorgeous omelettes of yours, with the sun-dried tomatoes and goat cheese and all?"

"Sounds like you've given this some thought," I observed, and he sent me a look that said he had more on his mind than omelettes.

The rest of the drive home, we gossiped about various people from his office who'd been at the barbecue.

"Wilding looked good," Dan said. "I like those loose curls you put in her hair."

I sighed. "Wilding shouldn't need a perm to make herself feel attractive, Dan. I can't understand why she just doesn't go ahead and dump Eustis, after what he's put her through all these years!"

"They don't call him Tick for nothing," Dan muttered, flipping his windshield wipers on high as the rain started falling down harder. "You know what a tick does, Claire? It latches on and buries its head deep down, and sucks the blood out. Maybe Wilding understands you have to be real careful how you get rid of a tick. If you don't do it just right, part of that head stays put, just festering away, until you've got a nasty infection!" The downpour became a torrent, and Dan turned his full attention to navigating.

I thought a more accurate observation would have been that Wilding really had *two* ticks sucking her blood out, and concluded Angie Labiche must hold some kind of record for inflicting maximum damage in minimum time.

When we finally pulled into my driveway, I had brooded myself onto the verge of a tantrum. The sight of a silver Alfa Romeo parked across the street was all it took to nudge me over the line.

While it was true enough that Wilding rarely drove the Alfa herself, opting for the black Mercedes wagon, it hadn't been Eustis's place to hand the keys over to Angie. Nevertheless, that's what he'd done.

Why was she here, and how had she gotten in? All my pent-up animosity toward Angie came churning out, and I wrenched my door open almost before Dan stopped the car, ready to do I don't know what, but he caught my arm in a grip of steel.

"Claire!" His voice cracked like a whip, and the red spots dancing before my eyes faded. Then he pulled me close and pressed his lips to my forehead. "Let me handle . . . whatever needs to be handled, okay?"

I nodded, and we got out of the car. I handed Dan my keys, but as he started to unlock the door, we heard a sliding, bumping noise, as if something heavy were being dragged across the floor. He raised a finger to his lips for silence and led the way inside.

The first thing we saw was a half-empty bottle of the special Pouilly-Fuissé I keep chilled in the downstairs refrigerator to serve clients, and two of my best wineglasses, standing on Renee's desk without even a napkin to protect the pine surface. The red spots flared up again.

Several wide, shallow cardboard boxes were stacked haphazardly on the coffee table, and to one side of the room, a large, nearly appliance-size carton sat on the floor, the fringed tapestry rug rucked up beneath it.

Completely unaware of our presence, Angie, in shorts and halter, emerged from her manicure room and began to tug the tall box toward her quarters.

When she looked up and saw us, she froze, just for an instant, then let go of the box, flashing Dan a brilliant smile as she hurried over to him, both hands outstretched.

"Ah, *mais oui*, Dan!" she chattered, rolling her eyes and

breasts at him. "You are so very . . . strong. You can help me move this so heavy, 'ow you say? *boîte.*"

"Oh, 'ow you say? Bullshit!" I snarled at her, not waiting for Dan's reaction. "Isn't it interesting the way your English plumb deserts you at the most convenient moments? Perhaps you'd care to explain what you're doing here. Better yet, how did you get in?"

Her dark eyes grew round and feigning hurt, she turned to Dan. "Dan, are you going to allow her to speak to me like that?" she demanded, pouting.

Outrage at her temerity rose in my throat like bile, until I saw that Dan was standing there, a massive brick wall, arms folded across his chest, staring at Angie grimly.

"Since this is the *lady's* home and place of business, and since you, *Miss Labiche,* are merely an employee, and it is outside business hours, which means you are trespassing, *Mrs. Claiborne* is well within her rights to insist you answer any and all questions she chooses to put to you!"

Angie jerked back as if he'd slapped her—something my own palms were fairly itching to do—as if she'd had every reason to expect him to back her up against me.

But I had finally gotten wise to Angie's clever little strategies. By implying Dan was betraying her, I was then supposed to think there was something for him to betray. It was a presumption designed to be flattering to the male involved, while, at the same time, undermining and threatening to the female.

But neither of us was playing. "Well?" Dan persisted. "How *did* you get in?"

Angie moved her shoulders in a Gallic shrug, which did double duty as a cleavage squeezer. "What is the mystery? I have observed where Claire hides a spare key in the doorknocker when she is possibly expecting a midnight caller, *hein?"* Angie smiled maliciously, thinking she had scored by insinuating I had a string of lovers trotting up the stairs after work.

It worried me that Angie had made it her business to monitor my movements so closely. "All right, we'll leave that for now," I said more calmly than I felt. "Just tell us what you've been doing here."

Before Angie could answer, Dan was stalking over to the box she'd been trying to move into her room, and ripped open the top. "Well, well, well!" he exclaimed. "What have we here?"

He began to lift out leather bags, of all shapes, sizes, and colors, tossing them carelessly onto the floor, while Angie darted about gathering them up, squealing like Mademoiselle Cochon.

I picked up a buttery silver quilted leather bag that looked just like a Chanel one of my girlfriends had bought in Paris.

Dan was inspecting a "Bisonte." "Well, whoever's doing this sure knows his business," he said. "See here, Claire? The buffalo's facing the opposite direction from the authentic one, and it's spelled "Bizonde." Very ingenious. That makes it barely legal, although I'm sure the Bisonte people would dispute that point."

Bag after bag, brand after brand, he demonstrated that somebody knew exactly how far they could go in each case. Fendi was spelled "Finde," and the stripes were reversed, while Judith Leiber was spelled "Judy Libre," and so on.

Dan turned to Angie, who was still clutching an armload of quilted bags to her chest, looking ready to spit bullets.

"Chanel," he remarked, "is always difficult because Coco Chanel herself is on record as saying that anyone who wanted to copy her designs was welcome. That freedom, however, does not extend to the 'double C' logo, or the name 'Chanel,' which is trademarked. Many cases have been fought on that very point."

But even there, the copyist had been circumspect. The two C's were back-to-back instead of interlocked, and Chanel was spelled "Channel."

During Dan's fascinating discourse, I noticed Angie's eyes shooting apprehensive little glances toward the pile of cartons on the table. I edged casually over until I was close enough, then whisked the lid off the top box.

Inside were watches of every description, all exact replicas of Rolex, Tiffany, Cartier, Patek, and the like. In this instance, the imitator had solved the trademark problem by simply omitting the names altogether.

Dan shook his head. Right in front of him, within smashing distance, was the mutual nightmare of a designer/manufacturer and a trademark attorney: perfect copies, technically not counterfeits, and therefore legal, if not moral.

"I wonder what other little surprises you've got in store for us?" Dan asked rhetorically, flipping the tops from box after box, each one holding watches, until the last four, which contained one-ounce spray bottles of rip-off perfumes, not the usual Opium or Giorgio "generic versions" but excellent copies of Givenchy, Cartier, Van Cleef and Arpels, Balmain, and Dior.

Dan was about to open the last two boxes when Angie shrieked, "Enough! Enough!" and burst into tears, allowing the bags she'd been holding to slip to the floor.

"Okay, are you satisfied?" she whined. "Humiliating me like this? Me, Angie Labiche, a poor little French immigrant manicurist trying to make it—"

Dan interrupted with a heartless laugh. "Let me tell you about this poor little manicurist, Claire. She was in charge of the entire Poire Gillaud Salon, until Madame Bertrand Gillaud happened to catch her giving poor old Bertrand the 'full treatment,' let's call it, in one of the private cubicles."

I made a heroic effort to suppress a snort of ironic mirth at Dan's righteous indignation. As if he hadn't been carrying on much the same way himself, less than a year ago!

But it was much more difficult to imagine rotund, apple-cheeked M. Bertrand, the stereotype of starchy French *bourgeois*, cavorting in buck-naked abandonment. Angie must exercise some special power over the turnip-shaped type. Look how she'd manipulated Eustis!

Unselfconsciously he went on. "Mathilde can be pretty *formidable*, as the French say, when her dander's up, which it sure was in this case. She found out that Miss Angie here was running a massage parlor after hours on the premises!

"After that, Angie not only couldn't get work at any other decent place in Paris, but Mathilde was hellbent on having Angie's esthetician's license revoked!"

Angie favored us with an evenly distributed glare of hatred. She must have realized right then Dan knew more than he was saying. "So?" she hissed. "What are you going to do?"

Dan grinned wickedly. "Oh, it's not Claire or me you have to worry about," he assured her, "it's the IRS. When they get a whiff of your undeclared cash—and believe me, they will, with no help from us—you'll be deported as an undesirable alien!"

Angie started to blubber again, picking up the two unopened boxes and clinging to them as if for strength. "It is only because I wished to make enough money to move away from Eustis's cottage. You have no idea how terrible it is there for me. Eustis has been so generous, but that insanely jealous wife of his treats me like dirt! I want to have my own little place, and on my small wages which you grudgingly pay me, I cannot accomplish this!"

"What are you talking about?" I demanded. "You keep seventy percent of what you earn. That's more than anybody else in town!"

Angie tossed her head. "Pah! I am worth more!"

"How much do you expect to make on all this stuff?" Dan asked thoughtfully.

She looked sullen. "Most of the bags were to fill orders I had already taken," she admitted. "With the watches and perfume, I am thinking well over fifteen thousand dollars. Of course, you will take a cut," she offered craftily.

"No, thank you!" I said tartly. "You can keep every cent of your ill-gotten gains, and welcome! I consider this my contribution to Wilding Keller's being rid of you at last.

"And by the way, it may interest you to know that Eustis doesn't own one stick of that real estate he's been so generous with. It all belongs to his wife!"

By her blank stare, I knew Angie hadn't understood that little detail.

Dan cleared his throat. "In order to protect yourself, Angie," he said in a gentler tone, "it would be very smart if you told us who all is behind this operation. It's got to be very big to encompass such a wide variety of goods, and extremely profitable to pay for such intricate legal advice to keep them just inside the line.

"But if they're willing to go this far, it won't be long before they'll cross that line and then, you'll be involved in real counterfeiting, which is a real crime."

Angie chuckled scornfully. "Oh, I am sooo scared!"

Dan shrugged. "Suit yourself. But nasty things can happen when counterfeiters fall out. I have personally witnessed some of them. Not a pretty sight, I promise you."

At that, a flash of fear crossed Angie's face, but she said nothing.

I became aware I was holding something, and it turned out to be that luscious quilted silver leather "Channel" shoulder bag. I recognized the symptoms. I was hooked.

Laughing, I said, "Allow me to be your first customer, Angie. Is this little number spoken for?"

Angie looked wary. "Ahh, no, I don't think so." Natural avarice flared in her pupils. "You can have that one for three hundred dollars."

"No way!" Dan stated flatly, pulling out a wad of bills that made Angie's jaw drop open. He peeled off a hundred dollars and held it out to her. "This is it, tops."

Angie's hand snaked out and grabbed the bill, and I cooed over my bag. It really was a beauty.

Finally, after hauling all her goods into her domain, with neither of us lifting a finger to assist, Angie got into Wilding's car and roared off into the night.

"Baby," Dan said. "I could really use that omelette now!"

"It's the least I can do." I smiled.

He grunted. "You can say that again!" And he chased me up the stairs.

Later, after locking the door behind him, I noticed the depleted bottle of Pouilly-Fuissé still on Renee's desk where Angie had left it, and carried it to the sink where I poured the dregs down the drain.

When I went back for the wineglasses, it suddenly struck me. There were two, and they had both been used. Who else had been here with Angie?

Chapter
13

*A*fter an embarrassing confrontation like the one Angie had experienced with us, she might have been expected to show a little less arrogance, a little more humility.

Not Angie Labiche! During the next three weeks, she was more brazen than ever, on top of which she seemed to be enormously excited about something.

Maybe it was merely the fact that most of her clients, looking slightly furtive, were leaving with pseudodesigner bags gingerly clutched in hands with freshly painted fingernails.

And, apparently, the cologne was going like hotcakes as well, judging by the haze that engulfed many of Angie's customers as they paused by Renee's desk to pay their official tabs, checking the time on their new ersatz watches. Since I had once sold the real thing, I was able to identify most of the clones, but the one that smelled best to me was whatever Mrs. Shelby Bell had purchased, something with a dry, fruity tang that seemed familiar.

Mrs. Shelby Bell, a former beauty queen, was filthy rich, very demanding, and stingy as they come, always trying to get me to knock something off the bill, frequently "forgetting" to tip Renee. Another one of Marcel's little bequests to me.

With her brunette coloring, big hair, and smart mouth,

she was like a Suzanne Sugarbaker from hell. In fact, Renee and I called her "Hell's Bell."

I'll say this for her, though. She had good taste and knew a bargain when she saw it, buying piles of Angie's wares every time she came in. Usually she loved to linger and talk, but when I asked what her fragrance was called, she'd snapped:

"How should I know? I can't read French!" and hurried off.

Perhaps Angie was so smug because hardly a day went by that Marcel didn't either send flowers or pull up in his maroon Corniche to take her to lunch or dinner. I could have warned her that this rush of attention was always a sure sign that Marcel was getting set to break off a relationship. As it turned out, however, she had already correctly interpreted the signals, and acted accordingly.

Then, one Saturday, as Marcel was letting Angie off at the shop after a long lunch, Eustis had shown up, radish-red and acting crazy.

Four women, heads adorned with wads of aluminum foil, plastic caps full of purple goo, odoriferous clumps of rollers, and other indignities so necessary to beauty, crowded around the window overlooking the street, avidly watching the drama unfold. They scattered, giggling, as Angie scrambled in, looking harassed and out of breath. She must have literally run up the steps in her four-inch heels.

I do remember thinking at the time that it was most unlike Angie to flee the scene of a conflict between two suitors. But I had no way of knowing she had just passed the point of no return.

When Angie disappeared into her room, I sneaked another glance through the window. Marcel and Eustis were talking, and they both looked dead serious.

A minute later Wilding drove up in her black Mercedes

wagon, idling in the middle of the street. I knew she didn't have an appointment today, so I waited to see what would happen next.

Wilding had apparently rolled down the passenger's window, because Eustis stepped off the curb and leaned inside to speak to her.

Marcel waved briefly to her, then climbed into his own car and drove off.

Eustis, after one last blind stare at the townhouse, opened the door to Wilding's wagon and got in.

The shrill beep of a client's timer called me back to duty, and I put the whole incident out of my mind until much later.

Dan was taking me to dinner, so I went upstairs a little early to shower and change, leaving Renee to clean up and do the laundry. It was nearly eight o'clock before I came back down.

I was just checking my reflection in the full-length mirror, thinking I looked pretty good in the short, cyclamen silk sheath with spaghetti straps and matching pumps, my hair tumbling loose, when I heard a sound.

"Renee?" I called tentatively. "Is that you?" I walked toward the kitchen, and realized the sound was coming from Angie's Parlor, as Dan and I now called it.

Her door was standing ajar, so I pushed it open and stuck my head in. Angie sprang forward, attempting to block my way, but I could see over her shoulder. There were several unopened boxes, the flat, wide kind that contained perfume or watches, on the floor. Business must have been even better than I thought, if she was already reordering. Evidently she had been preparing to hide them.

"What's the matter, Angie?" I teased. "No honor among thieves? Afraid somebody's going to swipe your *faux* finery?"

"Everybody has something to hide, *hein?*" Angie remarked offhandedly. "Like you, Claire, with your silly little key in a hollow angel.

"But even some *faux* things are far more valuable than others," she added cryptically.

Something in her voice made me look at Angie closely. She at once appeared glitteringly triumphant, and incredibly strained. Suddenly I felt very sorry for her.

"Angie—" I began impulsively.

Angie forestalled me, seeming to read my mind. She shook her dark head warningly. "No, Claire," she said simply but emphatically, with a shade of regret.

Then she acknowledged grudgingly, "You look . . . very nice tonight."

"Thank you," I said cautiously. "Dan is taking me to that new place on the river."

"Bon appetit!" Angie said, and shut the door in my face.

A moment later, I was still standing there, astonished, when Dan rang the bell. But as soon as I saw him, large and luminous in a crisp white linen suit, I forgot everything else.

"Ooh, Big Daddy!" I did my best Southern Belle squeal as he ran a slow, sensuous finger under one of my shoulder straps. "I can tell it's gonna be a long, hot summer!"

I'll always remember that night because we ate well, drank a lot of wine, danced, and ended up having a nightcap on the mezzanine of the Royal Orleans, where you will eventually see just about anybody if you sit there long enough.

In this case, Charlotte Dalton and Joey Antoine turned up, and we had a surprisingly pleasant couple of drinks with them. Dan drove me home, and after a dizzying session in the backseat of the BMW, he hustled me quickly to the door and kissed me goodnight. It was then almost 2:00 A.M.

✿   ✿   ✿

After an unaccustomed amount of booze, at such a late hour, I should've slept like a ton of bricks until noon. But, at about 3:30 A.M., a noise downstairs roused me.

Suddenly I sat bolt upright in bed, wide awake. I couldn't remember if I had ever taken the key out of the angel's wing. What an idiot I was! Angie could've told anybody, or even used it again herself.

I put on my slippers, stuck the portable phone into the deep pocket of my terry robe, and tiptoed to the landing, where I pushed a switch, flooding the entire shop area with light.

Carefully I descended the stairs, but when I slowly rounded the curve, I almost fell the rest of the way down when I looked over the banister into the wide foyer.

Angie Labiche was lying on her back, the pale gristle of her windpipe gleaming in the midst of a wide, red watermelon grin. Her throat had been sliced from ear to ear.

But what was worse, the man crouched by her body looking up at me, his white linen suit smeared with blood, was Dan.

Chapter

14

We stared at each other for the space of several heartbeats.

Dan, bleary-eyed and blue-jowled, his once-gorgeous linen suit resembling nothing so much as a pile of dirty laundry, looked pretty awful. But he most definitely did *not* look like a murderer.

As usual, Dan read my mind. Our self-imposed semi-celibacy was paying off. The faintest flicker of amusement crossed his face, then quickly faded. "Hell of a thing for a guy to trip over on his way to take a piss!"

I ignored his deliberate crudeness, which was completely out of character, and failed to conceal the quaver of horror in his voice. My feet came unglued from the step, and I proceeded to descend the staircase, noticing with strange detachment as I drew closer that, other than the congealed blood on Angie's neck and chest, there didn't seem to be any on the rug or the floor.

When I reached Dan, he rose from his crouch and looked down at me, searching my face for some kind of sign.

"Dan, I want to kiss you. Right now!" I announced.

Relief flared in his bloodshot eyes, even as he made a token protest. "Oh, baby! My mouth tastes like a buzzard's butt—"

I effectively silenced him by pulling his head to mine. He was right. His breath was indeed foul, so to speak, with garlic, alcohol, and cigars, but I didn't care because his lips were sweet and soft and loving. Not the kiss of a killer.

"Although I made myself face the possibility," I admitted. "And I kissed you because I wanted you to know absolutely where I stood, but mostly because I just plain old wanted to. You do strange things to me, Dan Louis."

"Honey, strange ain't the *word* for the things we're gonna do to each other," he promised, and made a move to touch my breast, only to jerk his hand quickly away. We had both noticed the blood on his sleeve at the same time.

"And strange ain't the word the cops are gonna use if they knew I was standing here with blood on me, fixing to grope you while Angie's lying there dead."

"Well, I certainly won't mention it," I promised, taking the portable phone from the pocket of my robe.

Dan reached for it. "I'll call headquarters," he began, but I was already punching in a number.

"You do realize," I reminded him, "that this is Joey Antoine's district. And since we were swilling down daiquiris with him and Charlotte not too many hours ago, he certainly won't be at headquarters."

"You still know his number by heart, huh?" Dan inquired, a little jealously.

"Don't be silly!" I scolded. "I'm calling Charlotte."

On the tenth ring, Charlotte finally answered. "This better be good," she snarled thickly.

"Well, 'good' is not the word I, personally, would use to describe this," I replied.

There was a groggy silence. "Claire? Issatshu? Whatsmatta?" she croaked.

"Plenty, I'm afraid, Charlo. Would you happen to have a policeman handy?"

She yawned hugely. "I would not. Like they say, you can never find a cop when you need one!"

"This isn't funny, Charlotte," I snapped.

She came awake instantly. "What's going on, Claire?" she demanded.

"I just found Angie dead in my shop. Murdered," I amplified.

"My God!" Charlotte squeaked. "How do you know?"

"Oh, no one special thing!" I said nastily. "Just a big old slashed throat, and . . ." I found myself staring with fascination at Angie's death wound. Seen up close, it looked more than ever like a wide, red grin. And all that white inside, now that could be the teeth . . .

Everything went black around the edges, and the room started to tilt. Dan caught me before I fell and picked up the phone from the tile floor, where I had dropped it with a crash. Faintly I could hear him saying something to Charlotte, then he severed the connection. I could hear him perfectly well when he asked, "Honey, are you all right?" But I couldn't seem to use my voice.

The next thing I knew, I was lying on my bed and Dan was pressing a cold damp cloth to my face. I sat up suddenly, and his tense expression relaxed. "Oh, baby! You really had me worried!"

I said the first thing that popped into my mind. "Dan, did you ever get a chance to use the facilities?"

He goggled blankly for a moment, then abruptly dashed back to the bathroom for some long-delayed relief. Afterward he stretched out on the bed beside me, saying he'd called the police. Then he started to talk about what had happened since we'd said goodnight.

"You know, I felt fine when we were driving home from the Vieux Carré, but after you went inside, I got back into the car, and wham! It hit me! Darlin', we drank two bottles of wine with dinner, and couple of brandies apiece at the restaurant tonight—I mean, last night. Plus all those daiquiris we had at the Royal Orleans. That's more booze than both of us put together ordinarily have in two weeks!"

So, he had wisely decided to simply sleep it off in the car, only to wake up with an urgent call to nature. Dan's an earthy guy in many ways, but he will opt for porcelain over petunias every time. He had retrieved the key from the angel's wing (God, how *could* I have left it there!) and headed in the dark for the downstairs powder room, only to stumble and fall right on top of Angie's body.

He shuddered. "I guess that's when I got the blood on me. And then the lights went on! For all I knew, it could've been the murderer who was coming down those stairs!

"Oh, Claire!" he cried, squeezing my hand so tightly, the big diamond ring nearly broke my skin. "I was scared shitless! Not for me, but see, finding Angie like that, I didn't know what might've happened to *you!*"

Dan grabbed me and held me close to his broad chest, and I could feel his heart hammering violently as he rocked us both back and forth. "I'da killed the sonofabitch with my bare hands if he'd hurt you!" he whispered fiercely, then kissed me with equal fierceness.

My robe had come untied, and the fragile lilac silk nightie which had been a part of my trousseau was no match for Dan's mouth and hands, which were suddenly everywhere. My skin melted like butter under his thick, hot fingers, and our craving was so intense, nothing short of the sudden scream of sirens that erupted down in the street and the urgent pounding on the front door could have stopped us then.

Dan groaned and heaved himself up from the bed. "Do

you think the Lord is trying to tell us something?" he inquired wryly.

He made hasty and largely futile adjustments to his clothing by the light shining in from the bathroom. He really was a mess. Unexpectedly, my heart gave a jolt of tenderness, and I felt tears welling up.

"I love you, Dan Louis Claiborne!" I called after him as he hurried out, and he gave me a quick smile over his shoulder.

I switched on the bedside lamp and sank back, succumbing to a spell of total inertia. A million jumbled thoughts shifted through my mind like kaleidoscope patterns. Angie's strange exultation . . . Eustis and Marcel arguing . . . Wilding picking up her husband like a little boy from school . . . Angie hiding things . . .

The noises and voices from below swelled in volume, and I decided I'd better go down. A glance at the state of my nightie propelled me to the closet for a pair of fleecy pink sweats. I didn't bother with shoes, just stuck on my bedroom slippers.

Once again I found myself peering over the stair railing. I studiously avoided the knot of people surrounding Angie's body. The scene was unpleasantly reminiscent of an army of ants scavenging a carcass. I couldn't see Dan anywhere.

"Isn't getting mixed up in murder way too *tacky* for a Junior League lady like you?" Joey Antoine mocked from the foot of the stairs. So Charlotte had notified him, probably thinking, in ignorance as I had, this would automatically be his case. However, none of us, not even Dan, was sufficiently familiar with police procedure to realize that's not how things were done.

In fact, Field Supervisor Captain Russo had already assigned someone else by the time Joey arrived on the scene.

And, though we didn't find this out until later, Russo only allowed him to remain on sufferance, in an "unofficial capacity," because he claimed that as a close family friend, we had requested him to stay.

Now I shot back at Joey, as I continued down the stairs, "You are absolutely right. Murder is way too tacky. I'll probably be blackballed!"

Although I did wonder why he wasn't actually doing anything beyond his usual self-appointed task of making everything as unpleasant as possible, I just took it for granted that Joey was in charge. At least a good, nasty fight with him would distract me from the grisly business going on in my precious little shop.

I still hadn't located Dan, and Joey said scornfully, "Don't bother looking for your bigshot ex-husband, Claire. He's being interrogated by Detective Sergeant Savoy. And if Mr. Society King thinks he can slide out of this mess by hitting on *her* like he does every other woman in this town, he's in for a big surprise!"

I stared at him. "Out of *what* mess?" I demanded.

"Oh, come on, Claire! That asshole's got blood all over him!"

"Because he fell on top of her!" I yelled angrily.

"Now that," Joey sneered, "sounds about right!"

Of course, Joey knew the story of "Dan and the Cheerleader." New Orleans is, after all, a very small town. But that wasn't what horrified me. It sounded like Joey was accusing Dan of murder.

As a Southern woman, I exercised my sacred privilege to cry, and was putting my heart into it when I felt a Kleenex pressed into my hand. It was from Charlotte, who'd entered unnoticed. From the look on her face, she'd overheard our whole exchange.

While I blew my nose, she stood with folded arms, regarding Joey in anger-charged silence.

He was delighted to have a new target. "Hey! What the hell are *you* doing here?" he demanded loudly.

Charlotte's paper-white skin tightened and her green eyes grew wide. It was clear he'd never spoken to her like that before.

"Why, hon! I'm here to do my job," she replied with deceptive calm. "Just like you!"

Joey glared at her in confusion, obviously unable to immediately recall exactly what Charlotte's job *was*. And when he did, his black brows drew together angrily. "Oh, no you don't! You get yourself on back home right this second, and I don't mean maybe!" he ordered in thunderous tones.

The extent of his chauvinism was astounding. Imagine thinking he could order an Emmy-winning reporter away from the scene of her own big scoop on a sensational murder story because she was his girlfriend!

The police personnel across the room were still going about their business, but their ears were flapping in our direction.

Charlotte's knuckles tightened around the unplugged WDSU microphone she was holding, but she tried to act as if Joey hadn't just made them both look like a horse's heinie.

"Claire, if you need me, I'll be outside with the crew," she said with dignity, and gave my arm a squeeze.

She started to turn away, when Dan entered from the direction of the kitchen, accompanied by a tall, blue-eyed woman with reddish-gold ringlets and skin the color of tea and milk.

I recognized the exquisite creature from the television news, being interviewed by Charlotte and others at crime scenes, but this was the first time I'd ever seen the legendary

Detective Sergeant Nectarine Savoy, NOPD, in glorious flesh.

Nectarine was her real name, but not the one intended by her mother, a New Orleans octoroon, who had been a Broadway chorus girl before her marriage to the scion of another old New Orleans octoroon family.

The Savoys had been driving through New England to enjoy the fall foliage, when the baby had arbitrarily decided to put in an appearance two weeks early. By the time the couple managed to locate a small hospital in rural New Hampshire, neither of them was very coherent.

The baby girl was born within half an hour of their arrival, so it fell to Mr. Savoy to cope with the paperwork, which was handled by a stolid, middle-age nurse.

Everybody knows about the lines drawn between black and white. But in some cases, there are even more definite demarcations between people of color.

Mr. Savoy was so anxious that the space "Race of Mother" not be filled in with just plain "Negro" that he kept babbling "She's an octoroon! She's an octoroon!"

The nurse, of course, had never head of such a thing as an octoroon. But the really funny part was, it never entered the minds of anyone at the hospital that the light-skinned, exotic-looking Savoys were Negroes. They all just took it for granted that the attractive pair with the charming accent were some kind of excitable foreigners, probably Eye-talians.

It sounded to the nurse as if Mr. Savoy, rendered hysterical by the birth of his first child, was saying "She'sa nectarine! She'sa Nectarine!" And she interpreted that to mean he wanted to name the little girl "Nectarine."

A couple of days later, as the three Savoys prepared to leave the hospital, they were presented with a birth certificate for Nectarine Savoy. Race: Italian!

Somehow, though, Nectarine seemed to fit the infant

perfectly, so the parents never bothered to change it. That name, and the hilarious story behind it, had gone a long way toward taking Nectarine Savoy to the top of the modeling profession during the late seventies and early eighties.

Then Nectarine's best friend, another famous model, had been brutally murdered, and the case was never solved. Nectarine resigned from Wilhemina's and came home to New Orleans, where she enrolled in the Police Academy.

Now, a few years later, she was rising to the top of her new profession. In fact, she was Joey's superior.

I noticed that Charlotte and Nectarine were eyeing each other warily, and I remembered Joey's bitter satisfaction when he said Dan wouldn't get anywhere with her. That sounded very much to me like the voice of a man who'd tried himself, and failed miserably.

Charlotte nodded a greeting. "Sergeant Savoy! I was just informing Sergeant Antoine that my crew is outside preparing to shoot. When you have sufficient information, perhaps *you'd* care to make a statement?"

Nectarine inclined her head. "Be glad to, Ms. Dalton. Especially since I'm in charge here." She paused. "My, my! You certainly managed to get onto this story in a hurry!" Savoy observed dryly, her luminous eyes shifting between Charlotte and Joey.

Joey's face turned the color of a kettle of cooked crawfish, and Charlotte smiled sweetly. "Well, that's what they pay me for, Sergeant Savoy. When you're ready for us, just whistle! We're never far away!"

Dan's path had been blocked by two enormous men, one black, one white, both clad in green scrubs, noisily wheeling a stretcher across the tile floor. Sergeant Savoy turned as he approached. "Mr. Claiborne, you've been very helpful. Thank you. If you'd be so kind as to come down and make a sworn statement, possibly tomorrow? Someone will notify you. You're free to go now."

Joey, who'd been seething with frustration, spoke up. "Excuse me, Sergeant Savoy. But isn't it customary for a suspect to be interrogated at headquarters? I'm only asking in my unofficial capacity, you understand," he drawled sarcastically.

If I had only known his "unofficial capacity" hinged upon his claim to close personal friendship with us, I could have saved us all a lot of trouble. At the time, it just sounded like so much police jargon. Nectarine Savoy's sapphire eyes flashed with astonishment as she looked from Joey, whose jaw was working with tension, to Dan, who shook his head slightly in disbelief.

"I was unaware that Mr. Claiborne was considered to be anything more than an important witness in this incident, Sergeant Antoine," she stated dismissively, no doubt thinking with a friend like this, we had no need of enemies!

"Well, that's probably because you are also unaware of the nature of the relationship between the victim and this . . . *important witness*, Sergeant Savoy," Joey retorted, just this side of insolence. "I'm just mentioning this in my unofficial capacity, mind you."

Sergeant Savoy drew herself up. "Sergeant Antoine! One more remark like that, and you won't have any capacity at all!" She threw an unmistakable double entendre in there, and several people nearby laughed.

Joey flushed, and stalked off angrily.

"Mrs. Claiborne?" Sergeant Savoy asked. "Will you please come with me? I've sort of taken over your kitchen as my base of operations here."

Reluctantly, I left Dan's side and followed her, but stopped in amazement as we passed Angie's room. The balloon shades were ripped from the windows, the sofas and windowseats had been slashed, and Angie's manicure table was overturned. Reeking, iridescent puddles of nail polish from broken bottles gleamed on the tiles. Three men were doing something inside.

I must have looked as sick as I felt, because Savoy said defensively, as she motioned for me to precede her through the swinging door that led to the kitchen, "Not our work, I assure you, Mrs. Claiborne."

I collapsed into a chair at one end of the antique pine table and thought longingly of coffee. Belatedly remembering my manners, I invited Sergeant Savoy to sit, before the ironic twitch of her gorgeous lips reminded me that this was not a social occasion.

I could almost hear her thinking "Even with a dead body in her front room, she's still acting like a Belle!"

"It's upstairs," I told her, watching her eyes wander around the kitchen.

She looked startled. "Pardon me?"

"If you were looking for my deviled egg plate, it's upstairs," I said with a straight face.

Sergeant Savoy burst into a brief but appreciative chuckle, and nodded her head. "You got me then, Mrs. Claiborne!"

Nectarine gave me another smile and began, "Now, Mrs. Claiborne." She paused. "May I call you Claire?"

I said yes, and she went on. "I'm going to ask you a few questions, make notes for my own reference, and then, tomorrow, I'm going to take a formal statement from you, with a police stenographer present. Do you consent?"

I laughed without amusement. "And if I said no? Please, Sergeant Savoy. Let's just get this over with." I didn't suggest I call her Nectarine.

"Fine," she said, pulling out an expensive-looking tan leather notebook and gold ballpoint pen, all business now. "When did you last see the victim alive?"

"Just before Dan—Mr. Claiborne—came to pick me up. It was a little after eight o'clock, because we had dinner reservations for eight-thirty at the new Italian place on the riverfront."

"Oh, you mean Largo? Isn't it fabulous!" Sergeant Savoy quickly caught herself. "I'm sorry. You stated you last saw the decedent at approximately eight o'clock. Aren't those pretty long hours for a beauty shop to be keeping on a hot summer Saturday night? Did Miss Labiche have a late appointment?"

"Sergeant Savoy, I have no idea. She handled her own appointments, so you'll have to check her book, if you can find it in that mess. I'd gone upstairs about six-thirty, after my last client, to get ready for my date." I almost giggled, referring to Dan as a "date."

"Renee Vermilion, my assistant, regularly remains until about seven-thirty P.M. on Saturdays." I broke off to give the sergeant Renee's address and telephone number. "Her duties are to sweep up, launder the smocks and towels, total the week's receipts, and prepare the bank deposit for me to make on Monday morning."

Sergeant Savoy nodded. "If this was a regular routine, isn't it possible that Miss Vermilion had been under observation for some time, and Miss Labiche was a victim in a burglary attempt?"

How to explain that if Angie Labiche had ever come across a burglary in progress, she would have been far more likely to demand a cut of the loot than jeopardize her skin to prevent it? Besides, it didn't explain the trashed room.

But I merely said, quite truthfully, "I never thought of that. But we can check the safe right now."

She smiled. "It's already been checked and found intact. Did you have any conversation with Miss Labiche?"

Again I told the literal truth. "Very little. She . . . complimented my outfit and wished me 'bon appetit.' " I swallowed hard, remembering that indeed those were Angie's very last words to me, maybe to anybody else on earth. Except the killer.

Savoy made another note to herself. "And did the decedent have any conversation with Mr. Claiborne at the time of his arrival?"

"No. Dan didn't even know she was still here, and I didn't think to mention it. She had . . . closed the door. I got the impression she was . . . rearranging her work area."

We both thought about the lovely room in tatters.

"Well, somebody certainly did," Savoy observed sourly, studying me. "And you returned from your evening out, I believe Mr. Claiborne said—" She flipped back a few pages in her notebook. "—around one-thirty A.M.?" I nodded.

She stared hard at me and her eyes glittered. "Then why did you wait until nearly four o'clock to report the murder?"

I felt myself blush. I didn't have any idea how Dan had, or even *if* he had, explained our unusual arrangement, but the only thing I could do was tell the truth about why he had been sleeping it off in the car, instead of upstairs with me, as unlikely as it sounded.

Savoy listened with a rapt expression, chin propped on one hand. I concluded by saying that I had gone directly upstairs, not bothering to turn on any lights until I reached my apartment, because I didn't need them. Therefore, even if Angie's body had been there, I wouldn't have seen it.

At any rate, the reason we hadn't reported Angie's demise for nearly two hours was because we hadn't known about it until Dan had crept in to go to the john and fallen down on top of her.

This, of course, necessitated my explaining about the door being on an air hinge, and the automatic deadbolt lock, which I always snapped on at around five-thirty every evening, and the spare key in the angel's wing. Not even Angie would've gone out and left the lock off if she'd planned to come back. Not that she gave a damn about my property, but she'd been plenty concerned enough about her own to try to conceal it. With good reason, it appeared.

No, if Angie had left and returned, she'd have used that key to get in. Or somebody else had used it. By the time I'd finished, a grey dawn was pushing through the French doors that opened onto a small flagstone area surrounded by the herb garden. Dan had laid it out himself, ordering special varieties of lavender plants from Grasse, which were blooming in fragrant profusion, along with thyme from Greece, English rosemary, and Italian basil.

Nectarine Savoy gazed outside for a few moments, then said apologetically, "I'm sorry to have to bring this up. But I must ask you about what Sergeant Antoine referred to as the 'nature of the relationship' between the victim and Mr. Claiborne."

All along, I had been unconsciously braced for that question. I shrugged. "Although you may not have gathered from his current appearance, Sergeant Savoy, Dan Claiborne is a very attractive man. Unfortunately, Angie Labiche mistook his kindness in hiring her on my behalf as an overture to closer contact, and behaved accordingly.

"It caused both Dan and myself a lot of embarrassment, because her pursuit of him was very public, and she tried to imply he returned her interest."

Savoy twirled her gold pen. "Well, why didn't you just

fire her then?" she asked indignantly. "I mean, this is your business, isn't it?"

I was on delicate ground here. I said, "Yes, and that's exactly why I didn't fire her! In the short time she was here, she had attracted a large following and made me a lot of money. I really couldn't afford to fire her at this point."

I leaned forward and confessed, woman to woman, "However, I was on the lookout for her replacement from Day One!" As we shared a knowing female chuckle, two thoughts struck me. I would certainly have to find another manicurist now. And also, without intending to, I had just established I had no motive for eliminating Angie. After all, why kill the goose that laid the golden eggs, even if she'd been trying to lay my husband as well?

At last, Savoy closed the notebook, then replaced it, along with the gold pen, in the large pocket of her brown silk jacket. Since she hadn't asked me anything about Eustis or Marcel, I knew Dan hadn't tried to defend himself by dragging their names in as having been involved with Angie. Most guys would have.

The swinging door burst open to admit a chunky, winded cop in uniform. "Sergeant Savoy! Come quick! They've just found the murder weapon!" he blurted excitedly.

Chapter

15

$\mathcal{I}$ was right at Savoy's Hermès heels as she rushed out to join a triumphant plainclothes detective standing just inside the door to Angie's "parlor." And, even before I actually saw the object he was brandishing in a white handkerchief, I had a terrible certainty I knew what it was.

Sure enough.

Savoy studied it with interest, then turned to me, delicate brows raised questioningly. "Do you recognize this, Mrs. Claiborne?"

I reflected that just moments ago, I had been "Claire."

"Yes," I admitted, my knees as well as my voice trembling, not only because of what the man was holding, but because I could now see into Angie's room. One section of wall bore a graffitilike bloodstain.

So this was where she had been killed. But how had her body gotten into the main work area?

"Mrs. Claiborne!" Savoy repeated impatiently.

I let out my breath. "Yes," I began again. "That is a straight-edged razor from Seville, Spain, circa 1790. It is part of a small collection of antique barbering equipment that was kept in an unlocked glass display case mounted on the wall to the right of the receptionist's desk."

I made it a museum guide's recital to keep myself from thinking about to what purpose that razor had been put, omitting the information that the collection had originally been started and neglected by Dan, who realized it would blend perfectly with the decor of Eclaire. The Spanish steel blade had been sharply honed, the silver handle brightly polished, and it was a cinch that, unless the killer had managed to wipe the thing completely clean, both Dan's and my prints would be somewhere on it.

Dan's full lips thinned to a tight, grim line when he saw the razor. He put his arm around my waist and drew me close.

Joey Antoine chose that moment to return, and when he saw the weapon he barked, "Where did you find this, Leo?"

Joey's question caused the officer some consternation. He looked around for Savoy, now standing in Angie's doorway, received no signal, and answered tonelessly that it had been shoved down into one of the conical holly bushes in the rose garden, which Angie's French doors opened onto. His hands bore the scratches to prove it.

Then Joey wondered aloud, in his "unofficial capacity," if anyone had ordered another search of the rose garden, earning a glare from Leo Wickes.

"Sergeant Antoine, Officer Wickes here has already initiated one successful search. And while I agree that it is a wise precaution to go over the area again in full daylight, may I ask just what you think we might discover?" Savoy inquired.

Joey blustered a little. "Well, uh—whatever the slasher wore, for one thing!" he finished challengingly.

"Whoever"—he started to slide his eyes in Dan's direction, but thought better of it—"did the job sure as hell got plenty of blood on him." He gestured at the red-splattered wall, which silently confirmed his statement. "Maybe he was just stupid enough to try to ditch something in the backyard.

"Hell," he went on, warming to his theory. "He could've even gotten away over the back wall!" Again Joey stopped just short of looking at Dan. "Assuming, of course, that he got away."

Savoy's mouth quirked. She, at least, had noted the eight-foot wall was topped by another four inches of broken glass, the New Orleans intruder deterrent of choice. Not very high tech or attractive, but oh, so effective!

When Savoy pointed this out to Joey, his ears reddened, but he quickly came back with, "Well, but there's a door in the far wall."

"Always kept locked," I replied to Savoy's question. "Only the poolman and gardener have keys."

Reluctantly, I gave her their names and numbers. Kevin, the poolman, an aging L.A. surfer acid casualty, I wasn't so concerned about. But Ogilvie, our treasured Scottish gardener, was another matter. A cranky old coot who could take offense at the most innocent question, Ogilvie's gentle artistry with roses had transformed the small, humdrum backyard into a microscopic Giverny.

He had worked for Dan's parents, among others, for years, and Rae Ellen would never forgive me if the temperamental Highlander took such umbrage to being questioned by the police that he washed his hands of the entire Claiborne family.

"Sure you don't have another key-carrying angel on *that* door, Claire? Shoot, we're gonna have to nickname you St. Peter, the way you pass out keys to this house!"

"Sergeant Antoine!" Savoy snapped. "That was completely uncalled for!"

Joey raised his hands in mock surrender. "Oh! Excuse the hell outta me, Sergeant!"

"Do you recognize the murder weapon, Mr. Claiborne?" Savoy asked.

Dan's arm tightened around me. "Certainly," he said

calmly. "It's from my collection of barber antiques, which Claire and I hung in the main salon."

Savoy looked at Officer Wickes, who shrugged, and went off to look at the display case. When he returned, he carefully addressed his remarks to what he considered to be a neutral point between the two sergeants. "The display cabinet is standing open. There is an empty space between some old moth-eaten shaving brush and a weird-looking pair of scissors.

"And it's already been printed," he added with a touch of irony. But Dan and I hadn't, and Joey derived great pleasure from watching us submit to the indignity.

Four uniformed cops entered from the yard through Angie's French doors. "Nothing, Sergeant Savoy," the spokesman reported. "Sergeant Antoine?" he added belatedly, in surprised confusion.

Savoy's ability to function had been severely impaired by being forced to tolerate Joey on the scene, whatever his capacity. Trying to run a murder investigation while steering a diplomatic course around Joey's childish outbursts in front of civilians was difficult enough. But his presence was causing uncertainty in subordinates who had worked under each of them separately.

But, unless he did something really awful, she couldn't override Captain Russo's permission for him to remain.

The two men who'd been busy in Angie's room, looking identical in baggy Matlock seersucker suits, came out, carrying heavy bags over their shoulders, and another officer put a seal on the door.

A bumpy rattle heralded the approach of the stretcher, bearing its mournful burden, and everybody stood aside respectfully as it passed. We still do that in the South.

A procession seemed to have formed, and was moving out the front door. The medical examiner and forensic cops followed the stretcher, then the uniformed officers, then Leo Wickes and another detective, then Sergeant Savoy.

I was eerily reminded of the joke about New Orleans' uncontrollable urge to put on a parade, told by the late local comedian, Billy Holliday.

He said, "If a bomb ever dropped on New Orleans, and there were only three people left, two of them would start parading down Bourbon Street, and the other one would be standing on the sidewalk yelling, 'Throw me somethin', Mister!'"

True to our roots, Dan and I automatically fell in, bringing up the rear, but halted at the top of the steps when we saw what was going on out there.

Down on the street, remote vans from the other two televisions stations had joined the one from WDSU, and their reporters were jostling for prominence.

Blue and white police cars, radios sputtering, were parked at random angles, blocking access to St. Charles Avenue from that direction, and a crowd of spectators, from bathrobed residents to early-morning joggers and dog walkers, mingled with stranded churchgoers, all swarming excitedly around their favorite reporters or gaping while the coroner's men loaded Angie into the back of their van.

We watched the circus for a few moments, then Dan took my hand to pull me back inside before the reporters spotted us, or some enterprising neighbor immortalized us on home video.

But our retreat was cut off by Joey Antoine, who was standing fists on hips, surveying the action with a wicked gleam in his eyes.

"You going the wrong direction, bubba!" Joey informed Dan.

Dan looked at him. "I don't think so," he contradicted, and made a move to pass, which Joey immediately blocked.

"I think Lawyer Dan oughta get a firsthand taste of how our criminal justice system works in the sovereign state of Louisiana," Joey said thoughtfully.

"If there were *really* criminal justice," I observed, "somebody would come along and lock *you* up, right this minute!"

Dan, who saw what was coming, sighed wearily and folded his arms. "You've got no evidence to arrest me, Joe."

Joey snapped, "That's Sergeant Antoine to you. And who said anything about arrest? But sure as God made green alligators, you are material witness material if I ever saw it. You own the murder weapon, you got the victim's blood on you, and some people just might think you got a pretty good motive too! Shit, if you weren't who you are, you'd've been down at the station by now!"

Actually, he was probably right about that.

Suddenly I realized what Joey had in mind. I gasped. "Joey! You wouldn't dare! You just couldn't do that to Dan!"

Joey wavered for a moment, then his eyes fell on Charlo, who was interviewing Sergeant Savoy. His expression hardened.

"No? Watch me!" He took Dan's arm and pulled him down the steps toward the crowd. Dan told me later that he didn't bother to resist because he felt *sorry* for him!

"You want Claire to call you a lawyer? Or do you just plan to have yourself a big old fool for a client?" he taunted Dan, loudly enough to attract the attention of the Channel 4 reporter.

He had seen Joey coming with Dan in tow, but looked confused when Charlotte, not understanding what Joey was up to, but determined to ignore him, pointedly turned her back and continued talking to Savoy, who also wasn't aware of his game plan. The Channel 8 woman cast a doubtful eye at Charlotte, who remained elaborately disinterested, and followed suit. Soon both their camera crews were tracking alongside Joey.

"Too early to say, Dick," Joey responded, when the man wanted to know if there were any leads, and, "No comment at this time, Edie." He winked at the woman, who asked if Dan was a suspect.

When he signaled to a surprised uniformed officer to put Dan in the backseat of a blue and white squad car, I ran down the steps and across the lawn, feeling the dew soak through my satin house slippers. I ignored the sudden interest of the journalists as I rushed up to Joey and grabbed his arm.

"If you're taking Dan in, you've got to take me too!" I cried, a little melodramatically, but that's how I was feeling.

Joey looked around furtively. He seemed in a big hurry to get away. I found out why later. "Shut up, Claire!" he ordered through clenched teeth. "You're making a fool of yourself!"

"Yeah, well you're certainly the expert on that subject!" I spat at him, and turned to Dan, who was still standing outside the car, the uniformed cop being mesmerized by this soap opera.

"I'm coming with you," I told Dan, but he put a finger on my lips and shook his head.

"It'll be okay, baby."

"But, Dan!" I wailed. Then I remembered something else. "Do you still have the house key?"

He nodded. "In my pocket."

Oblivious to the surrounding chaos and whirring cameras, I stood on tiptoe for his kiss.

As he bent to climb into the car, I asked, "Dan, honey. What do you want me to do now?"

He cocked an eyebrow at me and gave a faint grin. "Call Dad!"

The cop closed the door on him and took his place in the driver's seat, his partner got into the passenger side, and they drove away, siren whooping, blue light flashing.

Belatedly I realized Joey wasn't with them. He had only created that terrible scene for publicity! I looked blindly around. If I had seen Joey at that moment, there's no telling what I would've done.

I started back to the house, the frivolous slippers sinking into the ground. I knew they were ruined, and I didn't care.

"Mrs. Claiborne, are you the owner of this house?"

"Is Eclaire named after you?"

"Hey, Claire Claiborne! What will this murder do to your business?"

"Was that your ex-husband they arrested just now?"

"What was he doing here? Did he spend the night?"

"Mrs. Claiborne! Is it true your husband was having an affair with the victim?"

The questions came at me from all directions, like buckshot, and I responded to them all with silence and a blank stare.

No doubt I would make my debut on the 6 o'clock news, long hair still in tangles from when I'd first awakened to find Dan in the ultimate compromising position, no makeup, and soaked slippers.

Somebody, Charlotte, grabbed my arm. She was boiling with fury.

Sergeant Savoy stood next to her, looking ready to pull out her pistol and fire a few rounds at anything that moved. She hadn't realized what Joey had done until Dan was already gone. "I'm sorry, Claire," she said, anger turning her skin a fascinating color. "I'll take care of this as soon as I get back to the station."

"I've got to get this footage over to my producer," Charlo hissed in my ear. "I'll be right back. Okay?"

I nodded and trudged up the steps into the now-silent house. My beautiful salon was in total shambles. Drawers pulled out, armoire doors standing open, cushions replaced haphazardly.

Flopping exhaustedly into Renee's chair, I picked up the phone on her desk and dialed the number for Dan's parents.

Rae Ellen answered, sounding mildly annoyed at such an early call on a Sunday morning.

"Uh—Rae Ellen? This is Claire."

Her tone did not immediately warm. "Yes, what is it, dear?"

I gave it to her, as briefly and unemotionally as possible.

"I see," she said, when I had run down. "Well, it's very fortunate you called when you did, Claire. D.L. was just getting ready to leave for his golf game."

I pictured Dave Louis as he came on the line, voice crackling with energy. It had been a bitter pill for such a dynamic man to accept the limitations of his illness, especially when the ravages it was inflicting upon his body were, as yet, invisible.

"Talk to me, girl!" he ordered, sounding so much like Dan, it was uncanny.

Dave Louis's quick lawyer mind extracted a substantially more detailed account than the one I'd given to Rae Ellen, and soon he had totally grasped the situation.

"I'll take care of it, darlin'," he assured me confidently. "And don't worry, Claire. That man of yours knows how to handle himself. Takes after me that way. I've seen him deal with a lot tougher characters than young Joe Antoine."

Then Dave Louis, despite his eagerness to leap into the fray on Dan's behalf, surprised me by lowering his voice and saying, "Sugar, don't mind Rae Ellen right now. We just got that fancy wedding invitation, and she's feeling a little miffed 'cause you didn't let her in on it." He chuckled and added, "I don't know exactly what you two have been getting up to, or who you think you're fooling. But you better believe, you ain't *never* fooled *me!*"

I believed him.

After I hung up, I felt as if a huge weight had been lifted from my head. D.L. was on the case!

I stood and stretched, then walked over to peer cautiously out the window. It was amazing. During the twenty minutes or so I had been on the phone, except for a few neighbors still chatting across the street, the circus had left town. For the moment, anyway. There was still going to be the aftermath of the evening news to contend with.

I glanced at the large Pierre Deux pewter clock atop one armoire: 8:30 and way past time for coffee.

I shot the deadbolt and went upstairs, resolutely blocking out visions of the mess below. When I reached my apartment, I saw that the door was standing ajar. I knew the police had searched up here too, and if they had left it in the same chaos as downstairs . . . Waves of bad temper and frustration washed over me. I flung the door open so hard, it crashed into the wall and bounced back off.

My mood did not improve at the sight of Joey Antoine, standing in the arch between the living room and dining area, right hand resting casually inside his coat. I hated him at that moment.

"You won't need your gun, Officer," I jeered. "Or, on

second thought, maybe you will!" I let my eyes dwell wistfully on the heavy nickel and brass fireplace tools.

Joey began defensively, "Now, Claire, I know you're upset, but—"

"Then you don't know jack!" I cut him off. "Upset doesn't even begin to cover it. I am outraged, infuriated, and totally offended to discover you lurking around in my private living quarters!" I turned my back on him and headed for the kitchen, but he dogged my steps.

"I'm looking for the killer's coverup," Joey said. "Hell, Claire! You think the slasher would give seven shits about hiding it in your private living quarters?"

"Savoy already searched my place," I pointed out acidly. "You think she missed something?"

His face darkened. "Bitch!" he muttered under his breath, referring to Savoy, or me, or possibly both of us.

"Well, I'm just flat amazed you didn't find a big old pair of bloodstained overalls under my camisoles!" I drawled sarcastically, proceeding to grind an enormous amount of the blackest coffee beans I could find in my freezer.

"Dammit, Claire!" Joey squirmed uncomfortably. "I know *you* didn't do it! And yeah, shit! I know Dan didn't either."

I carefully spooned the coffee into an unbleached filter and poured water into the well of the machine before I trusted myself to speak. "So it doesn't bother you at all that you used Dan to grab some limelight away from Savoy for yourself and, by golly, make him pay for being who he is at the same time!"

Joey ground his teeth. "Claire, you don't understand."

"I'm not interested in understanding you, Joey Antoine!" I raged at him over the hiss and bubble of brewing coffee. "And don't you dare try to sell me some convoluted TV cop plot that you used Dan as bait to trap the real murderer.

"*And* if you should ever wonder what the phrase 'grace under pressure' means, I call your attention to how Dan Louis Claiborne handled himself today!"

The shot told. Joey's face darkened. "Claire, he's not our kind! We were doing fine until he came along!"

I stared at him, aghast. "Are you back on *that?* Well, pardon me if I get a little crude here, Joey. But, as I recall, it was common knowledge that you were banging that red-headed waitress down at Toulouse's way before Dan ever showed up!

"Furthermore, I am not, and never have been, intellectually, emotionally, spiritually, or physically 'your kind.' And it is very interesting to hear that you think Dan had to reach so far down beneath himself to haul me up! If so, where does that leave you and Charlotte Dalton?"

He flushed. "That's different," he muttered.

"Oh, yes! It most absolutely *is* different!" I flung back. "Because you're trying to bring her down! That's what makes it different. What makes it *right!*"

I returned his glare blandly. "Well, Charlo will never sink so low, Joey, better believe it! In fact, what time do you have?"

He glanced reflexively at his watch. "Almost nine."

"Good! Charlotte will be here any minute now! I think this should make for an interesting philosophical discussion, don't you? The three of us, sitting around, drinking coffee and hashing out the fine points about how it's all right for a woman to marry outside her socioeconomic bracket, just so long as it's *lower!*"

But Joey wasn't listening. He yelped and headed out the door and down the stairs, fast as he could go.

Chapter

16

$\mathcal{I}$was curled up on the sofa, watching TV with the sound off, trying to work up the energy to walk to the kitchen for a second cup of coffee, when the doorbell chimed with Charlotte's private signal: two short rings, a pause, then one long ring.

I shuffled downstairs in my bare feet, seriously considering having a buzzer installed. I'd already done a week's worth of aerobics on those stairs today!

Charlotte had changed into tight, yellow ribbed stirrup pants, oversize matching sweatshirt, and ankle-high, olive-green quilted tennis shoes. She was carrying a huge, enticingly grease-spotted bag from Café du Monde.

My stomach rumbled at the sight. "Beignets!" I squealed joyfully, leading the way back up.

"You *have* got coffee," she stated flatly, in a tone that brooked no denial.

"Gallons," I promised.

Charlo shoved the bag at me and took off her sunglasses to view the living room. "This is the first chance I've had to see your new apartment, Claire. It's beautiful!"

I left her to look around while I went off to the kitchen.

First, I poured coffee from the machine's carafe into a tubby green and yellow French stoneware coffee pot, and got out two mugs and dessert plates that matched the pot, along with two green linen napkins. Then I lined a deep, oblong pewter bowl with a yellow linen napkin, and emptied the bag of fragrant, still-steaming beignets into it.

I arranged everything on the huge old silver butler's tray that had been a wedding gift, and carried it into the living room.

The green and yellow color scheme was selected to match Charlo's outfit, of course. Southern women tend toward compulsion when it comes to things like this, even if they're half dead.

Charlotte had taken my place on the sofa and was staring at the silent TV screen, feet propped on the large pine coffee table.

She tore her attention away long enough to express approval for the presentation.

"God, I love your coffee!" she declared, draining her cup and holding it out for a refill. "It's like that chili they advertise you can stand a fork up in!"

I sank grateful teeth into a beignet, sending puffs of powdered sugar in all directions. I hadn't eaten a bite since that big dinner Dan and I packed away at Largo's, and a whole lot had happened since then, to understate the case.

Charlo made room for me on the sofa, and we continued to eat messily. Beignets are not something you can be dainty with.

Onscreen, an attractive blond lady was standing behind a Lucite pulpit, gesturing earnestly.

Charlotte pointed and spoke through a mouthful of doughnut. "Boy, that Gloria Copeland is really something! I mean, you can just look at the woman and tell she's for real. And honey, when she gets to preaching, she could blow the roof off the Superdome! But is her husband threatened? No, ma'am! He just sits back and yells, 'Amen, baby! Preach it!' "

She gnawed another beignet enthusiastically. "And just *look* at her, Claire. She's gorgeous! She's elegant! The woman's wearing practically no makeup, if *any*, and her clothes are in perfect taste. That lady looks like she just stepped out of Neiman Marcus!

"Shoot, you could take her to Galitoire's, and she'd fit right in!"

Charlotte subsided and gloomily wiped powdered sugar from her fingers.

"Maybe that's what I should do," she brooded. "Dump reporting and become a lady TV evangelist! God knows I couldn't do worse than some of those men!"

She took a deep breath. "Or maybe I oughta just call up Gloria and ask her to fly down here to cast about twenty-six demons out of Joey!"

So now we were getting down to it.

I said consideringly, "From all I've seen so far today, that particular exorcism could pose quite a challenge. Even to Gloria Copeland!"

Charlotte looked over at me and frowned. "Claire, what was Joey like when you were going out with him?"

I'd been thinking about this for a while. "It's really hard to say, Charlo. We only dated, oh, I guess two months, tops. And, as I told you, we had absolutely nothing!"

Tears slid onto Charlotte's white cheeks. "Well, neither did we, as I've been finding out."

She turned to me. "Did he ever tell you anything about his background?"

"Not too much, no." I didn't want to add I hadn't been all that interested. "Just that his mother was Italian and his father was French."

Charlotte drained another cup of coffee before she spoke. "Make that, his mama was an unwed Italian girl, which is literally the kiss of death in a virginity-worshipping culture, and his daddy, well, you know what they say about Louisiana!"

" 'How do you know who your daddy is? Because your mama tells you so!' " we quoted together.

Charlotte went on. "Joey got the idea, from something his mother told him before she died two years back, that his father was—is, if he's still alive—an Uptown Man."

"Dear God!" I exclaimed involuntarily. "No wonder he's such a mess!"

I put my hand over my mouth. "Oh, I'm sorry, Charlotte!"

"Please!" she said. "You're right! He *is* a dysfunctional mess, and that's why I'm cutting my losses, while I'm still not too far behind. As of right now, you can call me 'codependent no more'!"

"Are you sure?" I asked cautiously.

Secretly, I was relieved. From what he'd put me through today, let alone Dan, I had a bad feeling we had only seen the tip of the iceberg.

Charlo dangled her soiled linen napkin. "May I blow my nose on this?" she asked, and gave a mighty honk. "Let's face it," she said. "Not only is changing him *not* my job, but I know for a fact he's already been scouting ahead, you get me?"

I did. "Nectarine Savoy."

Charlotte nodded. "The one and only. I gave her a ride today, and us girls let our hair down. She told me that ever since she got transferred to Joey's district, he's either been trying to sabotage her, or jump on her bones!"

My friend was showing rapid signs of recovery.

"And how does she feel about that?" I was curious, remembering all the tension between them.

Charlotte threw back her head and hooted. "Honey, that

woman has dated *billionaires* and *potentates*! But what's worse, she *outranks* him!

"If Joey Antoine got freaked when a little old swamp rat he used to date married Dan Claiborne, or felt inferior to a pitiful Georgia Baptist debutante, he ain't seen nothing yet!"

She wiped her eyes, half laughing, half crying.

"The Nectarine isn't about to louse up her career for a few rolls in the hay with some Y'aat who's going to turn around and try to do her in, after he's done her. I *promise* you!"

Charlotte blew her nose again vigorously. "Now! Let's discuss this murder business!"

After I told her everything I could remember from my angle, Charlotte filled me in from her perspective, which included exclusive information gleaned from Savoy while the other reporters had been lured away by Joey's grandstand play.

There had been no sign of forced entry, meaning either the killer had known about the key, or Angie had admitted him herself.

No sign of a struggle either, which seemed to indicate he had plenty of time to protect his clothing, remove the razor from its niche, and come up behind her.

Angie hadn't been afraid of her killer. Or hadn't known he was there.

There was no clue as to what the slasher had been searching for, judging by the type of damage inflicted upon the room.

Suddenly I heard Angie's voice saying "Even some *faux* things are more valuable than others."

Although Charlotte knew all about Angie's moonlighting, I wasn't ready to discuss our last encounter until I had a chance to talk it over with Dan.

The only logical explanation for Angie's corpse having been shifted from the actual place of death, then abandoned, was that the killer planned, for some unknown reason, to remove her from the house. Then he had either changed his mind, or was interrupted in the process.

Which meant the killer might have been right there when Dan brought me home! If he had, and I had happened to turn on the downstairs lights, I could at this moment be lying next to Angie in an icebox with a tag on my toe.

After Charlotte left, I tried to call Marcel, but there was no answer, not even the machine. I seemed to remember that every now and then during the summer, he took his kids for a long weekend at his place in Covington.

Eustis I didn't even attempt to reach.

I cleaned up the mess Charlo and I had made, then, after one last effort to get Marcel, I switched on my own answering machine and embarked upon an elaborate toilette.

The original owners had gone all out on the master bathroom, the only totally modern area of the house. It was done completely in shades of grey, from fixtures to tile. The bathing area itself did retain one older feature, which had probably been installed in the thirties or forties. Instead of a single vertical showerhead, there were eight adjustable water jets, four on each side, placed at various heights.

One step down brought you into a long, shallow, recessed depression that could be filled and used as a tub, if desired.

The jets were at one end, and a tiled shower seat was at the other. On the wall between was a wonderful touch, built-in tile shelves for shampoo, bath oil, soaps, sponges.

I turned the water on, as hot as I could take it. Even in the summer, I liked a steamy bathroom. Standing in the jet sprays until my skin turned pink, I worked my way through every botanical product on the shelves, from shampoo to bath oil, and the air grew redolent with the scent of herbs and flowers.

I had just rinsed out the last bit of conditioner from my long hair, a tricky business, when I noticed that Dan had materialized from nowhere and was sitting on the shower seat.

I moved toward him as in a dream, perfumed vapors wafting around me.

Dan was bent over, elbows propped on knees, face buried in his hands.

Without a word, I squeezed shampoo onto his hair and began to lather, gently at first, then with more vigor. I noticed, with a little pang, a few threads of silver mixed in with the dark brown, and wondered why I'd never shampooed him before, or offered to give him a haircut, and why he'd never asked. Presumably, he was happy with Pierre at Distingué, where he'd been going for years, but still . . .

My hands moved down to massage his tense neck and shoulders, and I felt him begin to relax by degrees. I pulled him to the jets so he could rinse out the suds, then motioned him back to the shower seat. Because suddenly I knew just what to do.

After slicking conditioner through his hair, I steamed a washcloth and pressed it against his face, to prepare it for the exfoliant scrub, which I rubbed into the skin with firm, circular motions, as if I could erase those new lines of stress and fatigue with my bare hands.

When I had wiped the scrub away, I spread a tingling gel on his cheeks and carefully began to shave him. I had never, ever, shaved a man in my entire life, yet I found myself doing so now, with nearly mystical skill and precision.

While Dan was washing out the conditioner, I took a sea

sponge and fragrant soap, and started lathering him thoroughly, big chest to just below the belly; shoulders and back to midway down his fine, solid butt.

Kneeling, I worked the sponge from his well-kept feet, up the thick, muscular calves and powerful thighs, again stopping just short.

Something very strange was happening to me. There I was, dripping wet and stark naked, doing things for a man it had never entered my mind to do, and I was suddenly overcome with maidenly confusion at the mere thought of washing him *there*!

Silently, Dan took the sponge from my hand and finished the job for himself, his eyes never leaving mine. It was unbelievably erotic.

By the time he tossed the sponge aside and pulled me down next to him on the shower seat, I was literally dizzy with desire. But at the last moment, he moved away and said sharply, "No, baby! We've gotten this far and we're gonna wait if it kills us!

"And my God!" He groaned as his gaze swept over my moisture-beaded bareness. "I'm beginning to think it just *might*!"

Before he realized what I was up to, I had turned on the cold water and aimed a jet straight at him, full blast! Dan jumped to his feet with a roar and pushed me into the icy stream.

We clowned around until the cold shower had served its historical purpose, and I knew we'd just crossed some kind of cosmic bridge together.

And burned it behind us.

Chapter
17

$\mathcal{W}$e shared an icy bottle of white wine, while Dan got his first haircut from me. I could tell, from watching his expression in the bathroom mirror, that he was pretty impressed with my work, and I enjoyed showing off. His hair was thick and straight, and I loved the way it felt in my hands, seeming to take on a life of its own, yielding to fall exactly as I wanted.

Dan took to my pampering like a duck to water, and again I reproached myself for never having tried to discover what special little attentions he longed for from me. Where had I been?

I lingered over the cut, and Dan filled me in on what had happened when he arrived at police headquarters.

In a way, it had been kind of funny. Nobody was expecting him, so there was a lot of confusion. Neither Joey Antoine nor Nectarine Savoy had shown up yet, but eventually Captain Russo had been located.

Russo, who wisely remained noncommittal, kept Dan waiting in his office until Joey finally returned.

Technically, Joey had been telling the truth when he said we had requested his presence. Dan had to acknowledge that we (he was too much of a gentleman to blame me) had tried to reach Joey first.

But Joey's little stunt with Dan, which would have been overlooked only if Dan had been a serious suspect, and maybe not even then, was borderline actionable, especially since he admitted he never thought Dan was guilty in the first place!

He had just seen his big chance to score off Savoy, and grabbed it. He'd wanted not only to garner himself some television publicity, but planned to claim that she had neglected to collect important physical evidence, which, in fact, she had—Dan's bloodstained jacket.

But Captain Russo, after speaking to Savoy and Wickes and some other personnel who'd been on the scene to testify to Joey's insubordinate and obstructive behavior, had shouldered much of the blame, for not getting our confirmation that Joey's nonofficial presence was specifically desired and requested.

Sergeant Savoy had been chastised, and Sergeant Antoine had been forbidden any further involvement in any way, with any facet of the case. It's a good thing they hadn't known about how Joey had sneaked up to search my apartment, or he would have probably been suspended.

Into the midst of this debacle the district attorney himself, decked out in natty golf attire, stormed in and demanded to know on what grounds Dan was being detained.

"Guess who's part of Dad's regular Sunday foursome?" Dan chuckled.

With profuse apologies for the "inconvenience," Captain Russo sent Dan off in the same squad car that had delivered him to headquarters. Dan said the fascinated driver and his partner kept sneaking glances at him in the rearview mirror.

We were both pleased at how Dan's hair turned out, and I thought that Pierre had better look to his laurels, or Eclaire would be gaining a client.

Exhaustion finally caught up with us as we finished off the wine. Collapsing across the bed, we fell asleep almost instantly, snuggled together like puppies.

❀   ❀   ❀

"Better run, baby!" Dan warned, when we woke up at 4 o'clock, ravenous in every way. "This thing fires real bullets!"

The next best activity, of course, was to eat. Taking mental inventory of my refrigerator, I remembered the thick porterhouse steaks I'd bought a couple of days ago and, fortunately, not put into the freezer.

Dan volunteered to cook them. There was just one problem. He didn't have a stitch to put on! The first thing he'd done when he'd gotten back from the police station was to strip down and stuff everything he'd been wearing, except his shoes, and the bloody jacket (which now reposed in a plastic bag in the evidence room) into the trash compactor downstairs. Even his socks and underwear!

"I just wanted to get rid of it," he said ruefully. "I wasn't even thinking about what I'd wear later!"

"By the way," he added. "I had to load a new bag into that contraption. I guess the cops took away the used one."

It was chilling to think of somebody going through my garbage. Looking for a bloodstained whatever, I supposed.

I tried to imagine how they'd manage to sort through the compressed mass of hair, plastic caps, cotton, tissue, foil, end papers, and latex gloves. Presumably forensic science had kept pace with the technology of domestic appliances.

A thought struck me. It would have been ridiculously simple for the killer to utilize a pair of my disposable gloves. In fact, he, or she, probably had done exactly that. But even if the murder gloves were among the discards, how would they be able to tell?

My more immediate concern was Dan's sartorial needs. I was about to suggest I drive over to Octavia Street and bring back a few things, when I remembered something that made me break into giggles.

"Think it's funny, do you?" Dan inquired menacingly. "Well, laugh while you can, little lady! 'The boss' will remember this!"

Since I'd introduced Dan to Hugo Boss cologne, "the boss" had assumed very special significance to us. The identity of "the boss" had nothing to do with Bruce Springsteen. Or even Hugo.

"Promises, promises!" I teased. "I was only laughing because I just thought of something I've got available for you to put on! I was saving it for the Big Night, but—" Still chuckling, I took the gift-wrapped package from a bureau drawer and gave it to him.

When he had opened it, he stared at the contents in disbelief, then erupted into gleeful hoots. "Oh, you nasty, *nasty* woman!" he sputtered. "Where on earth did you *get* these?"

He held up the white Lycra briefs, the fly of which had been embellished with a big red valentine, edged in white lace, and bearing the inscription: BE MINE.

There was something missing, though.

"But you have to supply your own arrows," I informed him demurely.

Dan gave me a pulse-pounding look. "Don't you worry, darlin'. There ain't going to be no shortage in the arrow department!"

When he put the underwear on, we started laughing again.

"You rascal! You're just full of surprises, aren't you?" Dan said, in a pleased way.

Then I recalled I had a few of his T-shirts (still my favorite sleepwear, silk nighties notwithstanding) and a pair of his sweat socks that had stowed away in the boxes he'd brought over from Octavia Street.

In a short time, Dan was reasonably decent, and he sat on the edge of the bed watching me slip into a pair of baggy khaki shorts and soft knit custard-colored tank top.

"Speaking of valentines, you know what would look real good on you, Claire? One of those pavé diamond hearts you can wear all the time."

The moment had come to let Dan know something. Walking over to where he sat, I stood and wrapped my arms around his neck. "As nice as that sounds, the only heart I'm really interested in is yours, Dan Louis. Oh, I admit, I love how you spoil me with all those play pretties. But if you didn't have doo-squat, you're still the only man in the world for me."

He was watching me intently, and I went on.

"Charlotte once joked that you'd spoiled me for anybody else. She meant sexually, of course. And she was dead right. There just isn't anything possible beyond what we've got. But it's true in another sense as well. You have totally spoiled me for anybody else, ever, in any way."

When I finished, he pulled me close and buried his face between my breasts.

"Claire, you couldn't possibly know," he said in a muffled voice, "how much I needed to hear those words from you just now."

We had a blast fixing dinner together, another thing we'd never gotten around to doing before. Dan put on a long striped apron and kept flashing his valentine at me from under it.

While I cut up a baguette to make croutons, he set the steaks to marinate in a mixture of balsamic vinegar, extra virgin olive oil, and brandy.

The menu was simple. Steak, french fries, and Caesar salad with plenty of garlic and anchovies.

I hadn't known french fries were one of Dan's specialties, and was duly impressed at his expertise in turning them out in small, crisp batches of golden brown without smoking up the kitchen.

I told him everything that had transpired with Joey, and how Charlo had decided to end their relationship. Plus what she'd revealed to me about his unknown father.

"Ah-ha!" Dan exclaimed, putting a fresh paper towel on top of another lawyer. "That *does* clear up a lot for me!"

"Exactly!" I agreed. "All that time he was complaining about being forced to spend time with the likes of you, he was probably wondering whether you could be his cousin, or something, and if so, where was his share of the loot!"

Dan stuck a french fry into my mouth. "How flattering. But there's no Antoines in the Claiborne family. Was that the man's first or last name?"

"Charlotte says he doesn't know. But he's positive about the Antoine part. And that he's got a French background."

Dan pensively mixed us a dark rum and Coke apiece. "It shouldn't be too hard to track him down," he said at last.

I couldn't believe it! "You mean, you'd do that for Joey? After today?"

Dan shrugged. "Why not? A man has a right to know who his daddy was, even if this is Louisiana. And you never can tell. Maybe by now the old bastard is wondering whatever happened to the young one."

I was quiet as I used a pestle on garlic and anchovies in the bottom of a big wooden bowl. Dan had said *I* was full of surprises, but I didn't think I could hold a candle to him! Maybe this was what a marriage made in heaven was supposed to be, one partner constantly surprising the other with who they are.

When Dan bent over to check the steaks, coated thickly

with crushed garlic and coarse black pepper sizzling under the broiler, I couldn't resist pinching his behind.

He laid out plain white china and stainless flatware on the kitchen table, and I tossed romaine leaves and croutons through the rich dressing.

It was a shame to waste such good food on the 6 o'clock news, which we watched on the small Sony I keep in the kitchen. As it turned out, however, though bad enough, it wasn't nearly as awful as we'd expected.

We switched around all three channels to try to catch as many versions as possible. It was soon clear that the Channel 4 and Channel 8 reporters, as a result of having been deceived by Joey's grandstanding, were reduced to padding their insubstantial accounts with tabloidish references to "wealthy society attorney and his estranged wife" or "killer beast strikes in trendy beauty parlor" and the like.

There was Dan, looking decidedly seedy and disreputable alongside dapper Sergeant Antoine, and a mercifully brief flicker of myself kissing Dan, looking just a tad depraved with my snarled and tousled blond mane and bedroom slippers. I must confess, if we hadn't been the subjects my appetite would've been whetted, the human capacity to feast on tastily dished dirt being so sadly infinite.

Charlotte Dalton's report, by contrast, focused on the investigative aspects, and Sergeant Savoy looked both stunning and powerful as she crisply summarized the situation.

Charlo, while not above throwing in a few sensational allusions to "attractive French manicurist" and "popular uptown beauty spot," stressed the sudden intrusion of violence and tragedy, presenting it almost like a sober sort of whodunit.

There was not a single mention of Dan and me by name. After the news, we had coffee and strawberries with

Grand Marnier in the living room, while we watched *60 Minutes* and *Murder She Wrote*, both of which seemed pretty tame after what we'd been through.

Reluctantly I went to check the answering machine. Red light blinking furiously, it was predictably so clogged with messages that the tape had run out. Most of them were from seriously concerned friends and clients, but there were several from reporters, a couple of cranks, and one from Renee, volunteering to come in tomorrow, her usual day off.

The only call I returned was to Renee, who sounded alert and important about being questioned by the police, and I accepted her offer. I made a list of the others for her to handle tomorrow and went back to sit with Dan, who was looking preoccupied.

"You know something strange, Dan?" I said, when I'd gotten his attention. "There wasn't one call from Eustis or Marcel. I'm sure they've both heard about this by now."

Dan was surprised. "That is a little weird, isn't it? And speaking of phone calls, I better contact Leighton right away to let him know what the hell's going on. Incidentally, isn't it Juanita's day tomorrow?"

I had completely forgotten about Juanita Valle, who was the exuberant Cuban "household help" shared among Dan, myself, and two other families. Large and muscular, Juanita was excellent, even meticulous, in her work, but all the mess downstairs, in addition to the regular apartment cleaning, was far beyond even her heroic efforts.

Dan decided instead to call in the Krewe of Kleanup, the "industrial-strength" team they used at Blanchard, Smithson, Callant and Claiborne, to tackle the chaos.

"I'll phone Juanita and tell her to take the day off with pay. That okay, sweetheart?" Dan asked, making notes to himself.

I sighed luxuriously. Let other women rant and rave about not needing a man to handle things. I loved how Dan just took charge. Of course, he did it right, never neglecting to consult me, or defer if I objected.

Dan went on. "And guess what? I just remembered I have an old pair of sweatpants in the trunk of the car. Would you mind running down and getting them for me? I don't want to take a chance driving home like this!" He cast an impish eye down at his heart-shaped fly.

"Suppose I get stopped? Can't you just imagine what a field day the press would have! Something like 'witness in bloody slasher case jailed as flasher!'"

Dan tossed me his car keys when I brought him the portable phone on my way downstairs.

I left the automatic lock on, but flipped down the door-stop with my toe to prop the heavy door open. The air had cooled down, and it was good to get outside for a bit. In the distance, clangs and rattles from St. Charles streetcars mingled with blasts and honks from a variety of river traffic.

I went down the side steps that led to the stone portico where the BMW was parked. The street appeared deserted. Amazing when I recalled the madhouse it had been this morning. I cringed to think of Ogilvie's reaction when he saw how the front lawn had been trampled.

The sweatpants were lurking beneath a tennis racquet and golf umbrella in the far righthand corner of the trunk. There was also a pair of running shoes, so I took those too. It was unexpectedly messy in there, and I poked around for a few minutes by the automatic light that came on when the lid was lifted, like in a refrigerator. The trunk seemed to serve mainly as a locker for odds and ends of Dan's athletic equipment, mixed in with jumper cables and emergency items. There was a football, of course, and brightly colored golf tees scattered on the floor, a can of tennis balls, a worn catcher's mitt and a handball glove, the latter curled in such a way as to look rather suggestive.

Naturally, I couldn't resist investigating further. If I hadn't leaned in closer to see better at that moment, the blow would have been much harder. Or maybe it wasn't intended to kill.

Whatever the case, I barely registered the merest rustle in the tall oleanders that screened my property from the house next door, then a terrible pain burst behind my left ear. Then nothing at all.

Chapter

18

The four faces of Dr. Winters, my gynecologist, jiggled up and down in front of my eyes like frames of film caught in a projector.

It was very confusing.

"Did we have a boy or a girl?" I demanded, wondering why my tongue felt so fuzzy. " 'D' is for Dade," I murmured dreamily, suddenly picturing a chunky little boy with heavy brows and bright blue eyes and cowboy boots.

"Dade Louis Claiborne! Somebody make a note of that!" I struggled to sit up, anxious that my orders be carried out immediately, but gentle hands pushed me back.

Now multiple Dans swam into view. I smiled. There couldn't be too many for me.

"Dade Louis. Isn't that a great name, honey?" I insisted.

He leaned close. "It's perfect, darling. But I'm afraid he's not here right now. In fact, he hasn't even left the station."

Things were slowly coming into focus. The crackle of a paper sheet beneath me. A sink. A blood pressure machine. A bank of flickering monitors, emitting blips and beeps. Uh-huh. An encore performance at Touro Infirmary.

"What happened?" I inquired, with great originality. At least I knew it wasn't a miscarriage this time.

Dr. Winters answered. "Dan brought you in about half an hour ago, Claire. Somebody clubbed you in the head."

Now that he mentioned it, I could feel the pounding ache at the back and to the left of my skull. But I was still puzzled. Why was an ob/gyn on a head case?

"I had just come out of the delivery room when I saw Dan carry you in through Emergency," Dr. Winters explained. "My immediate thought was that it was another—" He broke off, then went on. "Anyway, I rushed over to find out, and when Dan told me what happened, I threw my weight around to cut through the red tape."

Dr. Winters had then routed his neurosurgeon squash buddy, Dr. Falk, from a nap in the doctor's lounge, and here we all were.

Nothing, not even beating drums and dancing naked around campfires, can compete with sports for the kind of male bonding that results in good, old-fashioned practical pull.

Dan and Bill Winters regularly faced off in the Doctors vs. Lawyers touch football games, and now, thanks to squash, my reflexes were being tested by none other than Dr. Frederick Falk, Touro's Chief of Neurosurgery.

When Dr. Falk, a stern-looking, rawboned gentleman in his early fifties, had finished with me in a prone position, he assisted me in sitting up on the edge of the table.

Dan and Dr. Winters shuffled anxiously in the background while Dr. Falk examined my injury, determining no skin was broken (so my attacker must've used his fist), hammered my knees, ran sharp things over my palms and soles of my feet, flashed lights into my eyes, ears, and nose.

Finally, he pronounced me fit enough to go home, and I could sleep, as long as I remained in an upright position. There didn't seem to be any concussion, but that wouldn't be official until he got the skull X rays back tomorrow morning. When had they taken those?

After Dr. Falk had gone back to resume his nap, Dr. Winters's beeper went off, and Dan and I were left momentarily alone.

"Oh, God!" Dan kissed my forehead gingerly. "You poor baby! I feel like a fool for letting you go outside alone. I don't know why, but it didn't even occur to me that there could still be any danger, since—" His lips clamped shut on whatever he'd been about to say, and he began to tell me what happened.

He had been tied up on the phone with a predictably upset Leighton Blanchard for about ten minutes, then put in calls to the Krewe of Kleanup and Juanita.

"By the way," he interjected. "Juanita insists on coming in tomorrow to do the apartment. She says men who clean offices have no idea of how to properly care for a lady's home. She sounded like I was trying to deprive her of her God-given rights, instead of giving her a paid day off!"

When he'd finished with the telephone, he realized I'd been away almost twenty minutes. The strange thing was, though, he thought he'd remembered hearing the heavy front door swing shut some time before. Dan had stepped out onto the balcony to call me, looked down, seen me lying in the driveway, and come after me.

Pausing just long enough to haul on the sweatpants and running shoes which had scattered around me, he then burned rubber for Touro.

My mushy brain was making a valiant effort to rally. The only reason for somebody to be lurking around my house was because they wanted to get inside. Which meant something they wanted was there.

While they were trying to figure out how to get in, along I came like a woolly lamb, leaving the door wide open behind me.

"Dan, was the door ajar when you got downstairs?"

He frowned. "No. In fact, I can't believe I even remembered to grab your keys when I dashed out. But you did leave it open?" I nodded.

"Shit!" he exploded, pounding the wall with his fist.

Well, whoever it was would've had plenty of time to look for whatever it was by now. The only place they couldn't search again was Angie's room, which had a police seal on it.

Of course, between the killer and the police themselves, that room had already been turned inside out.

Dan was furious with himself. "Tomorrow, first thing, we're getting all the locks changed, Claire," he announced. "Front, back, upstairs, and even the garden door, I don't care if Ogilvie threatens to show us what a Scotsman wears under his kilt! And yeah, don't remind me, the barn door and the horse. But then, maybe the horse is still inside."

I remembered again what Angie had said, and repeated it now. "Some *faux* things are more valuable than others."

Dan halted in midpace. "What was that?"

I explained about my last conversation with Angie, and he listened attentively.

"Why are we still sitting here?" I whined. "I want to go home."

The answer came immediately.

"Mr. Claiborne! I got here as soon as I could!" Sergeant Savoy said as she strode regally into the cell-like room, followed by Leo Wickes, who looked decidedly put out.

Savoy inspected me in a concerned way. "Okay. Let's hear what happened."

Wickes, mouth skewed in a sour twist, scribbled first my story, then Dan's, in a notebook, shaking his head as if to say this was pretty much what he expected from us.

Savoy cocked her head at Dan, consideringly. "So you

don't think it was really an attack on Claire? I'm inclined to agree. Somebody just wanted a chance to get back inside the house, and you handed it to them on a silver platter, Claire."

She paused. "Does this latest event give either of you any new ideas about what they are looking for?"

"Not me," I denied, and Dan just shrugged.

"Hmmm." Savoy tapped a long, elegant sandal. "Well, Mr. Claiborne, if you've got a medical release, I suggest you drive Claire home now. Officer Wickes and I will be right behind you."

Dan drove the short distance to the house at a more sedate speed than usual, not just because there were cops tailing us, but so as not to cause sudden jolts to my head, which rested on his shoulder. His arm surrounded me protectively.

When we pulled into the driveway, Savoy and Wickes were already up the steps and at the door, guns drawn, before we had even gotten out of the car.

Savoy signaled for Dan to unlock the door, and Wickes kicked it open with a force I found difficult to reconcile with his sedentary appearance.

I flipped on all the light switches from the master control panel just inside the door, and leaned against Dan for support. We had been instructed to stay put until they finished checking out the salon area.

Everything appeared to be pretty much in order. If something was gone, if it was any messier, I couldn't tell.

There was nobody downstairs, but the two police officers motioned us to remain where we were while they went upstairs. Since Dan had left the apartment door open, there was no need to kick that one in. A few minutes later, Savoy called from the landing that we could come up now.

"Does anything look disturbed to you?" Wickes asked as we walked in.

I glanced around, and yes, there were definite indications that the place had been searched. At least, thank goodness, they hadn't made a shambles like they had done downstairs. Incredible how flexible one's criteria for thankfulness can become.

Some books had been removed from the shelves, my Queen Anne desk had been gone through, and kitchen cabinets stood open, as well as several bureau drawers. Even the medicine chest hadn't escaped inspection.

Nothing, however, that I could see, was missing. The only jewelry I had besides my ring and the diamond studs, which I was wearing, were the emeralds, some baroque pearls, and several gold bracelets. All were present and accounted for.

With the sergeant's permission, Dan went around, straightening everything, while I watched from where I had flopped on the sofa.

Both she and the detective had determined it was fruitless to take prints, unless we wanted to file a complaint for breaking and entering. We didn't.

Before they left, Savoy said, "Oh, yes. Regarding your sworn statements. Under the circumstances, I'll send somebody around in a couple of days to take them."

After they left, Dan put me to bed, helping me out of my clothes in a manner both tender and tantalizing, gently sliding another of his T-shirts from my stash over my head, personally selecting a pair of flowered cotton bikini panties.

He piled a bunch of pillows behind me, adjusting them until they were in the approximate position prescribed by Dr. Falk, then stripped off his own ragtag assortment of garments and climbed into bed. There was no question of him leaving me alone tonight.

Dan kissed me and we held hands, listening to the sounds of the river in the night. Just before I fell asleep, I heard him chuckle. "Dade Louis!"

Chapter

19

I smelled Juanita before I saw her, that unmistakable melange of Maja cologne, tortillas, onions, jalapeños, and a dash of pure female musk.

Opening my eyes, I looked up at her large, kindly, concerned face bending over me. Her pale olive skin was smooth, with a slightly oily sheen, and the unplucked brows were drawn together over soft, brown eyes. Juanita had never permitted me to trim her thick, black hair, which, when unbraided, hung down to nearly touch her generous buttocks, and had steadfastly resisted all attempts to wax either her eyebrows or that faint but discernible Valentino mustache, apparently attaching some sort of female macho to it.

For the rest, she had huge, round *mamacita* breasts, the kind that look like they could provide ample nourishment for every deprived infant within a square-mile radius. Her torso was comfortably padded, but not sloppy, and she had those slim, shapely calves and exquisitely turned ankles unique to certain Latin women. Juanita's legs always had the silky texture of being freshly shaven, but her armpits were turbulent with thick, black tufts, creating an alarming illusion that she carried two spare female parts, just in case. Which, I supposed, was the point, but it could be that I was just missing some esoteric cultural approach to body hair.

With all that large and lush womanhood, I had been

stunned at my first sight of Carlos Valle, her husband, a small, wiry guy with a slightly simian countenance. I tried to imagine them making love, and couldn't escape the image of the little fellow gloriously awash in a great, undulating bowl of Jell-O.

"*Señor* Dan wanted me to tell you that he was first going to his house, then to his office," Juanita informed me, while I eagerly drank down the delicious cocoa she'd brought in.

"He will telephone you later, *niña* Claire," she added, fluffing up my pillows. Juanita had never called me "*Señora* Claire," except in the presence of guests at the dinner parties Dan and I used to give. Would soon be giving again.

Satisfied that I was okay for the moment, Juanita wheeled in her cleaning supplies and began to tackle the bathroom, calling out to me how she had felt, what she had said, what Carlos had said, what her sisters, mother, and brothers had said, in response to the television news reports about Angie's slaying. She came to stand in the bathroom door.

"*¡Ay! Querida!* I felt such a flutter, right here!" She pressed a hand to where she imagined, somewhere beneath the mammary vastness, her heart was. "I was so angry when they showed *Señor* Dan being arrested! *¡Dios mío!* And then, like a miracle of God, the telephone rang and it is *Señor* Dan! Right after we had seen him arrested on the television!"

I explained that Dan hadn't really been arrested, but she wasn't appeased. How dare they insult him that way! But what had upset her nearly as much was Dan's suggestion that she not come in today, that since professional cleaners were already engaged to do the downstairs, they may as well do the upstairs too.

"As if I would abandon you, *niña!*" Juanita exclaimed, waving her cleaning cloth like a banner. "I told *Señor* Dan it was not possible for me to allow a bunch of men to touch your *casa*! And as for professional cleaners, hah! Who is more professional than I?" she demanded, turning back toward the bathroom. "However, I am glad it is not I who must clean downstairs today, particularly when those men with the new locks are making such a mess!" She shuddered delicately.

When she had finished in the bathroom, Juanita made me take a shower while she cleaned the bedroom and changed the sheets.

My head felt pretty good, hurting only when I bent my neck down.

I came out, wearing the same T-shirt and panties I had slept in, but Juanita put her hands on her hips and clucked disapprovingly.

"That is not what a lady wears when she is confined to her bed!" was her verdict, and proceeded to select an outfit she deemed suitable. Soon I was reclining between clean linen sheets, propped up by a mound of freshly plumped pillows, attired in blue silk pajamas and a quilted yellow bed jacket.

"You've been watching too many reruns of *Designing Women*," I told her as she completed dusting, humming contentedly, having enforced her will.

When she left to finish cleaning the apartment, I closed my eyes and half dozed. Terrible thoughts and images began to run through my mind, that my attacker had been Dan. After all, he had sent me down to his car. Maybe it was so he could go through the apartment. Okay, he had made those calls, but, with a portable phone, it is possible to accomplish any number of activities while sustaining conversation. I personally had permed one entire side of a client's hair while, via portable phone, I attempted to persuade another that it would be a big mistake for her to go red.

All right. Worst case scenario: Dan was the one who

searched the apartment. But why hit me? I would never have been the wiser. Well, to try to point the cops in another direction. But to do that would mean he had killed Angie, after all.

At the sound of a low, distressed moan, I jerked awake, and realized it was coming from me. Angrily I banished the insidious demon whispers against Dan. There was no way he was capable of such hideous things. I had made my commitment to trust him, and that was that.

I drifted off again, but this time, the images were of Dan and me engaged in erotic activities, flashes of lips, tongues, and teeth, and his thighs with all that dark, luscious abundance between.

An insistent tapping drummed its way into my consciousness, and I surfaced reluctantly.

Renee Vermilion, my assistant, stood in the doorway, clutching my *Poire et Grappe*–covered appointment book, and both business and private portable phones.

"Oh, hi, Renee. Come on in," I said, motioning her to pull up the big chintz armchair closer to the bed, so she could use my nightstand for a desk.

She was dressed for combat in her burgundy, green, and gold-striped Eclaire smock, over black T-shirt and knee-length leggings. Black-and-gold El Vaquero cowboy boots completed the ensemble.

Renee was a real, 100 percent Cajun from Houma, Louisiana, with artfully tousled brown curls and bright dark eyes set like buttons in her sweet rosy face.

"Oh, Claire, *chér!*" she exclaimed sympathetically as she got herself settled in. "Juanita told me what happened when I got here. And then two real cute cops showed up and took some kind of thing off Angie's door . . ." Rene swallowed, and I knew she'd seen inside.

She recovered quickly. "No sooner had they gone when a big Krewe of Kleanup van pulled into the driveway, and a bunch of guys swarmed in."

Renee dimpled, going on to say that Juanita had immediately started telling everybody exactly what to do. In the midst of the ensuing tumult, people from the perpetually feuding draper's and upholsterer's had arrived and carted away the damaged shades and furniture. More of Dan's doing, no doubt. He thought of everything. My God, what a man!

Naturally, Renee couldn't focus on work until I had supplied a firsthand account. Her excitement dimmed a bit when she heard the more graphic details, but not for long.

"I'm sorry Angie got killed," she said seriously. "But I never really like her, Claire, no. She was sneaky and pushy and mean, and I don't care who knows I said so!" She tossed her curls defiantly and I recalled Angie had hit on Renee's boyfriend, a hulking second-string linebacker for the Saints.

"And you know what, Claire?" Renee leaned forward. "I think she was up to something strange. Saturday night, after I finished with the laundry, I walked into the salon and Angie was fiddling with one of those Ambrose Xavier portraits. She kinda jumped when she saw me, but then right away started making derogatory comments about Beaudine." Beaudine was Renee's linebacker.

"She had a felt-tip pen, and I figured she'd been drawing mustaches or something on the paintings, she was jealous as a motheroo of you, *chér*, but I checked after she went back to her room and they looked fine to me."

Renee paused for breath. "And that's the last time I ever saw her," she finished slowly.

I asked Renee if anybody had come in before she left, and she shook her head. "The police asked me that, and also if I thought anybody was already in Angie's office. And there wasn't, because I popped inside on my way out to the salon, just before I saw her with the pictures."

Renee looked a little guilty. "I was just going to borrow that nail polish, remember that color I like so much?"

I certainly did. Angie carried a line of French polish that even Marcel was unable to come by, and Renee had gone nuts over one particular pink. Not only had Angie declined to give Renee a manicure, saying she was just "the help" (it galled her enough to have to do me), she would not even allow her to borrow the polish. Moreover, she had flatly refused to order another bottle for Renee.

"Anyway," Renee said, cheeks flushed, "that's how I for true know that nobody was in there when I left."

I looked at her. "But you did get the polish." She nodded, displaying her nails, which glowed with a soft peach-pink, like the inside of a seashell.

"But I brought it back today."

"It's yours, sweetie," I told her, and she smiled gratefully.

At last we were able to get down to business, first working our way through the list of messages she had noted from the machine. A few were from reporters, but most of today's were from suppliers, wanting to know how many bottles of this or cases of that I would require when they delivered this week, questions that could not yet be answered.

We were going to have to close down for at least the rest of the week, possibly even through next weekend. Who, under those circumstances, would stick with Eclaire, and who wouldn't? And where on earth was I going to find another manicurist as good as Angie?

I sent Renee off to start calling all my scheduled appointments and sound them out, instructing her to make written notes of their responses. Also, to check and see if Angie's appointment book was anywhere around, and if it was, to do the same with her clients, saying that we expected to have a new manicurist available in two weeks, and they would be notified. If the book wasn't here, then she was to call Sergeant Savoy and ask when we could get it back.

I retained my private phone, and toyed with it, thinking.

Should I call Dan and discuss possible approaches for Eclaire to take? I ignored Gloria Steinem's wagging finger. I had no pride of gender when it came to whose idea worked best. Who cared? In the end, though, I didn't call him, not because of any feminist fundamentalism, but because I realized he was probably up to his neck in his own problems right now.

Instead, I called Marcel Barrineau.

Monday is traditionally dark for certain professions, including the beauty trade. It's our Sunday, in effect, when we rest, catch up on our grocery shopping, browse through the beauty supply stores for the latest products, even get our own hair done.

I tried Marcel's house first. There was still no answer, but I knew he'd been home since last night because now the machine was on. I didn't leave a message.

Next I called all four Salons de Marcel, and the institute, also getting machines. Then I remembered Marcel had once given me his private office number at the school when he still entertained high hopes of my eventual surrender. Closing my eyes, I tried to conjure up the seven digits, varying the rhythm. Twice I thought I had it, but one number did not exist and the other belonged to an incredibly hostile woman.

On the third try, I got him.

"Hello?" Marcel's voice was low and cautious.

"Marcel, it's Claire. I've been worried sick about you. Where have you been?"

"My God!" Marcel cried. "Am I not to be allowed to mourn little Angie in peace, even for one moment? Even here, in my private place, you all track me down, badgering me!" he wailed melodramatically.

"Marcel, you may not realize it, but I have been through a pretty grim ordeal myself since Saturday night. I fully expected to hear from you the minute you got the bad news. After all, Dan and I found . . . her."

There was a silence. "I am sorry, Claire," he said finally. "It is just that this is all so terrible. I was, I was, ah, out of town and, ah, only this morning I heard . . ." He trailed off. By his fragmented statements, I knew he was either under great emotional strain or lying. Possibly both. It was very likely he had indeed slipped out of the city for a clandestine adventure with some pretty little student, and he was feeling guilty.

"When did you last see Angie?" I asked curiously.

"Friday night," he fired back quickly, as if he'd been waiting for the question. "But why are you cross-examining me, Claire? Have I not had to endure enough of that from the police already?"

"Marcel," I interjected. "I didn't mean—"

But he paid no attention, bent on airing his grievances. "My God, twice in one day! First from that rather incredible-looking woman named Peach—"

"Nectarine," I corrected.

"Yes, yes!" Marcel was impatient. "You know her? Is she married? Never mind!" he snapped, as if I had been trying to press information on him.

"And then, not two hours later, another one, a man this time! Very intense!"

That would not be a word I would apply to Officer Leo Wickes. Dogged, persistent, and determined, yes. But intense?

"They are certainly hiring very good-looking police these days," Marcel allowed judiciously.

Definitely not Officer Wickes, then. An awful thought occurred to me. Even before Marcel uttered his next words, I knew.

"I thought he looked familiar," Marcel went on, "and it turns out he was at your party, Claire, monopolizing that lovely reporter friend of yours."

"Sergeant Antoine." I sighed in resignation. "What did he want to know, Marcel?" I was trying to postpone the moment of telling him that Joey Antoine was not on the case.

"Oh, much the same things as the Apple woman. What was your relationship, when did you see her last, and all. But Sergeant Antoine even brought up that ridiculous gossip about Dan. Strange he didn't seem to know anything about Eustis," Marcel observed with malice.

"But he does now," I said with certainty.

"Oh, yes," Marcel returned smoothly. "Sergeant Antoine seems like a fine young man," he continued. "After he had asked all his police questions, he wanted to know about my business, how I got started, all about my family. I also made a few suggestions about his hair. And Wednesday he is coming in for a cut."

Good grief. I didn't know what Joey was up to, but I did know he made it a point never to patronize what he referred to as "sissy hairstylists." I decided to just stay out of it.

Meanwhile, in a roundabout way, Marcel was bringing the conversation back to Sergeant Savoy, calling her "Plum" this time. As I reminded him it was Nectarine, which he very well knew, I reflected that he certainly didn't seem to be

exactly broken up with grief over Angie, as he had first protested.

"Marcel!" I cut in sharply on his ode to "Mango," as she
had become. "I need a good manicurist fast. Do you have one
in your stable to spare?"

He grew businesslike. "Not in your league, Claire. Those
I must reserve for myself. We are, after all, competitors!
Seriously, there is nobody who would suit. But I will keep my
eyes open."

I thanked him and was about to hang up when he said,
"Ah, Claire? As you know, I was very fond of Angie. Is there
maybe something, a memento, I could keep? Perhaps, even a,
uh, package or letter addressed to me? It is my birthday soon,
and she had hinted . . ."

I replied carefully that I didn't think so, but maybe the
cleaners would unearth something. "But, isn't it more likely,
if it was a personal gift, it would still be in her house on
Wilding's property?" I probed artlessly.

"No, I already looked there," Marcel returned, a beat
before he realized what he had revealed. "I must go now,
Claire!" he said abruptly, and disconnected.

Chapter

20

*J*uanita tromped in a while later, bearing a bed tray that held two steaming bowls of black bean and pork soup, fragrant with cilantro and cumin, her own special recipe.

"*Señor* Dan's favorite, remember, *niña*?" Juanita spread a large napkin across my chest to protect the precious bed jacket. "It will give you strength, *sí*?" She flexed a rocklike bicep by way of demonstration.

Renee followed close behind, reading glasses in screaming orange frames perched atop her head, ballpoint pen behind one ear, carrying a legal pad covered with scrawls. She sank into the chair, saying "Umm, that smells so good, Juanita!"

Juanita replied that it *was* good, and waited until we had sampled it and duly exclaimed. Then she marched out, Valentino mustache quivering with pleasure, calling back over her shoulder to let her know if we wanted more.

Renee was eager to make her report, but it had to wait until we worked halfway through the rich, delicious soup, accompanied by soft, buttered tortillas. I hadn't been aware of feeling so weak and hungry. That conversation with Marcel had taken more out of me than I realized.

Renee had been able to reach all but a few clients and, sliding her Day-Glo glasses down onto her pert nose, gave me the results of her telephone poll.

"Claire, everybody panicked because they thought you might be planning to close Eclaire! Practically all of them *swore* allegiance to you for true, and said they'd only go to Marcel or John Jay or somebody if they couldn't stand themselves any longer!"

Proudly she flourished the notations she'd made next to each client's name. Some amounted to rave reviews.

Renee didn't mention the ones who complimented her on her own great shampoos and scalp massages, skill and cheerful attitude. I was very pleased at how she was working out, not merely teachable, but able to implement what she'd been taught, acting as my third and fourth arms in tricky timing situations, such as perms, weaving, and color. You never knew what hair might do, and it was vital to have somebody who knew how to shift into red alert at the first alarm.

As soon as she got her license, I would put both of us to the ultimate test, by requiring her to cut my hair and renew the highlights Marcel added to my natural gold every couple of months. Once you have worked successfully on your own employer's hair, not even the most difficult and critical clients can faze you.

"So," I summed up when Renee had finished, "we're still in the hair business, anyway. But what about Angie's customers?"

Renee shrugged, waggling her hand from side to side. "That was kind of *comme ci, comme ca*," she admitted. "There's a lot of good enough manicurists in town, *chér*. People only start getting real picky when it comes to special things like hot paraffin treatments, and acrylics, or the perfect French tips, or pedicures. But, Angie was not only great at all those things, let's face it, she had a gimmick, being French and all. That's why nobody complained about her prices, which were almost twice as much as anybody else in town. It was prestige, you know?"

"Hmm. Well, I'm not exactly sure where that leaves us," I said. "Either we find somebody incredible within the next two weeks and keep the services and price structure as is, minus a one-time ten percent discount which I would gladly eat. Or get somebody 'good enough,' which means we eliminate the more esoteric things and lower the prices."

Renee looked at me. "There is one more choice, *chér,*" she advised. "I can take over until we find exactly the right person. I enjoy the work and I can do all that stuff Angie did. I'm really good, Claire, really!" She displayed her ten flawless nails again. "See? I even do my own acrylics."

I studied her hopeful face. It was the perfect solution. Personally, I couldn't understand anyone liking that exacting, tedious work. Nipping at cuticles is not exactly brain surgery, but it created extreme anxiety in me. Manicure/Pedicure had been the only low score on my state boards.

I asked how it had been left with the clients, and she said she'd promised to send out cards notifying them of Angie's replacement.

I pondered a few minutes, scribbled something down on my note pad, then passed it to Renee.

To Eclaire's Valued Clients:

Miss Renee Vermilion
will be offering full nail services
at special rates for a limited time only.

"Gosh!" she breathed. "Thanks, Claire!"

"Good, that's settled. Now, you better take care of the

banking. Just drop these off at the printer's on your way, Renee. Tell him to use the Eclaire tapestry-bordered post-cards with the angel, full mailing list, ASAP.

"But, remember, *chér*," I warned. "Hair takes priority. You've got to schedule all nail appointments around me."

"Will do!" Renee saluted, grinning.

When Juanita came to take the tray, they went out together, Renee wheedling for the soup recipe.

My eyelids felt like lead again, but this time it was a real sleep, with no dreams, either hellish or heavenly, and I didn't wake up until the telephone rang at about three o'clock or so. When I answered, Juanita had already picked up in the kitchen, and Renee from the living room.

Dan was laughing. "What a gratifying response!"

The other two got off the line, and Dan asked how I was feeling.

"A little decadent," I replied. "And getting antsy. I'm not used to lying around in bed all day. I'm going to try to get up soon."

"Now you be careful, darlin'," Dan cautioned. "And if you start getting even the least bit woozy, you call Dr. Falk, hear me?"

I promised I would, then told him what Renee and I had accomplished regarding Eclaire.

"For somebody bedridden, you've really gotten a lot done today, lady," Dan observed. "I think that's a good plan about Renee." He paused, and only then did I sense his distraction.

"What's wrong, Dan?" I asked, and he let out his breath in a whoosh.

"I've been in a marathon partners' meeting with Leighton and the others," he began.

I grew indignant. "And they're giving you a hard time because of the murder? Well, let me—"

Dan cut in. "No, Claire. It's not that. Oh, they're concerned about the firm's reputation, all right, but not just because of me. Seems like Belinda and Foley just split up again, only this time it was real noisy, and permanent, thank God!"

Foley Callant, who was one or two years older than Dan, had been miserably married to Belinda, who was nearly my age, since she was nineteen. Eleven years later, she was still nineteen. Belinda was involved in the art world, always running off to have flings with her "discoveries." It was one of New Orleans' greatest unsolved mysteries why Foley, a sweet, handsome, sexy guy, had always taken her back.

But this time, she'd fallen for a young Native American potter, and had purchased a good deal of expensive home equipment so she could take private lessons from him. Foley had walked into his house to find them reenacting the famous scene from *Ghost* and promptly exploded, throwing her out for good.

Dan continued. "In my case, they are at least paying lip service to my innocence. So far, anyway. But then, we had the Review. Eustis got passed over again."

I wasn't exactly sure how to respond. Though it was a terrible situation for everybody concerned, Eustis had been on probation for several years. Either because of lack of talent, or expertise, or neglect, or all three, Eustis had not cut the mustard. According to Dan, nobody in the history of Blanchard, Smithson had been passed over for promotion four times.

"Does he know?"

Dan sighed. "Not yet. He hasn't been in all day, or even called in, and nobody's home. And guess who gets to break the news?"

"Oh, Dan. I'm so sorry." As awful as Eustis was, he and

Dan went back a long way. This would be a horrible experience for both of them. But there was worse.

"They want me to fire him, Claire. The comptroller has been secretly auditing his expense accounts for the past year. Eustis has ripped off the firm for about ten grand!"

"My God!" I exclaimed. "Like father, like son!"

Dan lowered his voice. "Fact is, this would've been the perfect out, if only it had happened earlier this year. They don't even know the half of it yet."

I didn't say anything. I knew he would tell me when he was ready. When he spoke again, he was almost back to normal.

"Anyway, what would you like me to bring home for dinner tonight?"

"Just you and your appetite." I laughed, glad to be able to give him some good news, however small. "Juanita cooked a big pot of your favorite soup, *Señor* Dan!"

"Now that's exactly what I need!" he said. "Get her to bake some jalapeño cornbread to go with it, okay, darlin'? And I'll pick up a couple of pints of sherbet from that little place on St. Anne. Tangerine and lemon to cut through the lard!"

I gave him an abbreviated version of my talk with Marcel, and he was very thoughtful when he hung up.

Almost immediately afterward, Dr. Falk's office called, pleased to inform me that my skull X rays showed no sign of concussion, but no alcohol or tranquilizers for another twenty-four hours.

Then somebody from Sergeant Savoy's office rang to say that the sergeant wished to schedule an appointment to take our formal statements at ten o'clock tomorrow morning.

I dressed in jeans and a big mustard-yellow shirt, a color that Charlo says looks fabulous on me but like baby doo on practically anybody else. Since my bedroom slippers were gone, I put on the next best thing, a pair of navy blue boat shoes with an elaborate crest.

Juanita was delighted to fill Dan's order for jalapeño cornbread, and immediately began banging open cabinets and refrigerator to assemble the makings. I sat at one end of the table, watching her whipping eggs within an inch of their lives in a big red bowl.

Suddenly she looked up and caught my eye. "*Señor* Dan was very lonely for you, *niña,*" she said. "Every week, after you lost the baby, I would come early and find him just sitting downstairs staring at nothing. And one morning, when you were in Haiti, he was crying, *niña* Claire."

She let that sink in and began to flog the eggs again. "It is important to forgive, and I know you have forgiven. Now all will be well again, *sí*?"

I smiled at her. "*Sí,* Juanita."

"*Bueno!*" She stirred chopped red bell peppers, jalapeños, and whole corn kernels into the batter. "I will also put in some chorizo!" she announced dramatically.

One of the Krewe knocked at the apartment door, to let me know they had finished the work, and would I please inspect.

The Krewe had done a first-rate job. The salon itself was glowing, the kitchen spotless. Without the balloon shades and sofa, though, Angie's room looked strange, almost unrecognizable, like a heavily made-up woman's face stripped bare of cosmetics. Gingerly I examined the wall where Angie's life had been splashed. Not even a trace remained. It was as if she had never been.

On the floor, a box was filled with odds and ends the cleaners salvaged from the debris: a leather case of manicure tools; some unbroken bottles of polish; pink foam toe separators; various pieces of equipment; and several flat boxes of perfume.

I called Renee to go through the stuff and pick out what she wanted, then have the cleaners haul the rest away.

As I walked back through the shop, I ran into the locksmith, who handed me a ring of keys fit for a jailer, and a bill to match. I reflected that things were getting back to normal amazingly fast.

That was approximately eight hours or so before Joey Antoine was murdered.

$\mathcal{T}$wo short rings. A pause. One long ring. Two short. Pause. One long. The strident tones cut into my consciousness.

Dan bolted from bed. "What's happening?" he demanded wildly, not sure where he was for a minute.

The bedside clock's fluorescent dial glowed 2:10 A.M. The sound clamored again.

"Oh, God. It's Charlotte!" I said. I threw on my bathrobe and made for the stairs, Dan calling he'd be right there. Fear rose in my throat. This was totally unlike Charlotte. Either she was very, very drunk, or something was very, very wrong.

She wasn't drunk.

"Oh, God! Claire!" she gasped, not so much walking in as moving forward in a series of little jerks. Charlotte was dressed for work—that is, for the camera—in tailored black, hair and makeup impeccable. Her tawny lipstick stood out like a gash in an otherwise totally white face. She looked almost like a mime.

I eased her down onto the nearest sofa, and she struggled for speech. "In the warehouse district, on, on, on—Tchoupitoulous," she managed to squeeze out. "A story." She nodded emphatically several times. "Murder," she added as Dan entered, chastely clad in some sweats he'd brought over, among other wardrobe items, from Octavia Street.

His sudden appearance made Charlotte jump, and she

began to cry. "Claire, Dan. It was Joey! Joey's dead, dead, dead!" she wailed.

Dan and I looked at each other in shock while Charlotte went on, her words tumbling over each other.

She had anchored the 11 o'clock news that night, filling in for one of the regulars, so when the call came in about a homicide down on the docks, she was instantly available.

Charlotte and her crew arrived to find the area a madhouse, crawling with cops of every rank, from captain on down. She had plunged into the throng, asking questions of everybody she encountered, dockhands, derelicts, and police brass alike. The proliferation of cops was soon explained by the fact that the victim was an off-duty police officer. Two drunks kept following Charlotte around, trying to tell some hazy tale of limousines in the night, but, after her first initial interest, she decided they had confused reality with the plot of some dimly recalled movie.

The victim had been stabbed in the back in a narrow alleyway between two buildings. The crime was reported by a private security guard who was on his rounds outside one of the warehouses. Police were engaged in a search of the surrounding area, including some of the other buildings, but it seemed likely the killer had escaped.

While time of death had not yet been officially determined, it had to have been during the forty-five minutes it took for the rent-a-cop to complete his circuit, putting it near midnight.

By then Charlotte had managed to belly her way forward right to the scene, only to be blocked at the entrance to the alley by a grim-faced Sergeant Savoy. "Don't go in there, Charlotte. Send your crew instead."

Naturally, Charlotte had bristled at this. As long as reporters were allowed such close proximity to the scene, she wanted to be there. How dare Savoy treat her like some white wimp!

Little did she realize that Savoy was trying to protect her. Savoy, on the other hand, thought Charlotte already knew who the victim was, and couldn't understand her attitude, which was to blithely thank Savoy for her concern and sail right past.

Charlotte had been totally unprepared to see Joey Antoine lying there, blood all over his nice suede jacket, the hilt of an ordinary, untraceable hunting knife sticking from his back.

Only her rigid training kicking in had enabled Charlotte to complete her on-camera report about a young, off-duty cop mysteriously slain in the warehouse district.

Afterward she had ordered her crew to take the footage back to the newsroom and tell the producer to edit it any way he wanted to, something unheard of for Charlotte.

Then she had proceeded nearly to pass out in Officer Wickes's arms. Savoy ordered Charlotte a cab on the police radio, and here she was.

The next ten minutes were as close as I ever plan to get to hell. Charlotte suddenly went completely out of control, stamping her feet, shrieking, moaning and sobbing, choking with rage and grief. Furious at herself for ever getting involved with Joey, hating him for how he'd been, how he'd refused to be any different, grieving for the loss of his life, however miserable, remorseful for allowing things to go unresolved after their last strife-filled encounter after Angie's death.

It took both Dan and me to restrain her, and she finally calmed down, occasionally breaking into a hiccup. I held her in my arms while Dan poured us all a much-needed brandy. Charlotte gulped hers straight down and threw her head back against the sofa cushions. A little color seeped into her face.

"Whew!" she exclaimed some minutes later. "My God! I'm sorry, guys."

She shook her head as if to clear it, and eventually we started discussing Joey's murder as objectively as possible. Which wasn't very.

Finally Dan asked, "What do you suppose he was doing down at the docks when he was off duty? Did Savoy mention if she thought the killing's related to some case he was working on?"

"You mean, like maybe he got a tip or something?" Charlotte frowned. "Sergeant Savoy didn't say one way or other, but it could be. He was obsessive about things, you know. I'm afraid it would be just like Joey to go barging in without backup, no matter how forbidden that is. Or it might not have had anything to do with police work. He could've been following up a lead on his major obsession."

Dan frowned. "I don't understand."

"Oh, you know." Charlotte interrupted herself to yawn, seeming embarrassed by the intrusion of such a mundane body function in such a serious situation. "His obsession to find his father. He kept records and everything, although I never saw them." She yawned again. "Gotta go," she said, and stood up, weaving slightly.

"I'll drive you, Charlotte," Dan offered, but Charlotte refused.

"No, thank you, Dan. I'll be okay. Really. You stay with Claire. Lovers should be together. But I—I need to be alone."

"Where do you think you're going, Charlotte?" I demanded. "You can't leave until we've called you a taxi."

Charlotte flung open the door and pointed to the cab idling at the curb. "I told him to wait," she giggled, verging on hysteria. "Why not? It's on the city!"

Somehow, we got her down the steps and into the cab.

Dan went around to the driver's side and leaned in. "I am a lawyer," he announced to the startled driver, whose framed license proclaimed to be Monroe P. Sylvester. "I have duly noted your name and vehicle number," he droned ominously. "If I don't receive a call from this lady within ten minutes, informing me that you have personally escorted her to her door and waited to see that she is safely inside, I will immediately get into my car, track you down, and whip your ass. You got that?"

Monroe P. Sylvester, who at first seemed inclined to debate the issue, took another look at Dan's size and decided against it. He acquiesced sullenly.

"Good," Dan said. "As long as we understand each other." Then he handed the driver a twenty-dollar bill. "For your trouble."

"Charlo, you heard Dan. Ten minutes," I repeated.

"After *that*? I wouldn't dare not!" she assured me, sagging wearily against the cracked vinyl upholstery.

Charlotte duly reported upon arrival at her riverfront apartment, but we were too wired to go back to sleep. Instead, I gave Dan a complete set of new keys (no nonsense about angel's wings this time) and took him on an inspection tour of the shop, pointing out things that still needed to be done. When we got to Angie's room, Dan gazed silently at the now-spotless wall.

I noticed details I had missed earlier, like the discreetly closed gap in the display of barber tools and that the tapestry rug had been shampooed. The Krewe of Kleanup cut no corners.

The softly glowing portraits on the wall caught my eye. An elegant, sleek-haired businessman reading a newspaper; four women of varying ages with styles that ranged from big to blunt to curly to short, holding a wineglass, a telephone, a kitten, and a pair of hand weights, respectively; and a younger guy with a Luke Perry *90210* cut, grinning from behind the wheel of a sports car.

I told Dan what Renee had said about Angie's strange actions, and we walked over to examine the Ambrose Xavier portraits more closely, but there was no damage that we could see.

All of a sudden I found myself growing sleepy again, and my head started to throb.

"You go on to bed, honey," Dan told me. "I'm still wound up pretty tight. I'll just sit down here and have another brandy, ease out a little, okay?"

He kissed me softly, and I left him there. When I looked down over the stair railing, he was again gazing thoughtfully at the portraits.

I crawled back into bed and was instantly gone, rousing only slightly when I thought I heard a car door slam, then again when Dan slid in beside me. He reached over and twisted a lock of my hair around his fingers, like a child seeking comfort, and we drifted off to sleep together.

Chapter

22

$\mathcal{I}$t was inevitable that our state of unwedded semibliss would hit a snag at some point, what with two murders, a violent assault, disrupted businesses and schedules, and the strain of thinking, without actually saying, that the killer must be someone we knew. Both victims were too close to home.

Dan and I were both snappish the next morning. Two straight nights filled with emergency room dramas and death and very little sleep are bound to take a toll. Things began to heat up with the discovery I had run out of coffee, an unprecedented event, so by the time the morning papers arrived, we were ripe for a blowup.

The *Times-Picayune* had run two paragraphs on page 4, discreetly worded, but there was a brief reference to Dan. The real shocker, however, was the cover of a local weekly that claims to be dedicated to art and entertainment, but is really mostly witty gossip about the people involved in same.

Naturally, when the gossip is about you, it doesn't seem quite so witty, and my first reaction was nearly equally divided between a sense of violation and lack of identification with the two people in the photo. For the first time, I realized how celebrities must feel, innocently standing in the grocery checkout, only to be confronted with their own faces leering out at them from beneath big black headlines.

My second thought was to burn the thing immediately,

before Dan could see it, but this was July in New Orleans and a fire in the fireplace would instantly raise suspicion as to my sanity, if nothing else.

His reaction was worse than I expected. The T-P item was bad enough, but in the glitzy blowup shot of us, laughing in evening clothes, taken soon after our marriage at some do or other, Dan's bow tie was slightly askew and he was looking at me lecherously, hand hovering close to my rather impressive decolletage. We looked like we'd just drunk a lot of champagne and were headed for the nearest bedroom. (We had and we were, but that's irrelevant.)

Actually, the picture was very good, which made the contrast of Angie's dour passport photo, inset in the upper right corner, all the more poignant.

The most awful part, though, was the headline:

UN, DEUX, TROIS! BIZARRE TRIANGLE
IN THE GARDEN DISTRICT!

The story, however, was something of an anticlimax, failing to live up to the headline foreplay. Predictably, they tried to turn poor Angie's tragedy into a "fatal attraction" thing, but weren't able to pull it off.

I wondered resentfully why they hadn't managed to unearth her involvement with Marcel and Eustis, since they were digging up so much dirt. Both men were just as "Garden District" as Dan. Plus, Marcel Barrineau was a notorious womanizer, and Eustis Keller's father had starred in one of New Orleans' major financial scandals, which was saying a lot. I guessed they just hadn't bothered to dig that far.

Anyway, Dan was furious. He had come out of the bedroom, looking ill-tempered and slightly worn, but splendid, in a new green linen suit from either Rubenstein's or Weinstein's (both excellent haberdashers enjoyed his patronage) to discover the coffee shortage, caught sight of the picture, and we proceeded to have one of the worst fights of our relationship.

Somehow, it had become all my fault for having my picture taken with my boobs hanging out. I shot back that he could hardly object since he had been snapped in the process of grabbing them, and what's more, he had picked out that dress himself. Not only that, he was the one who'd hired Angie against my wishes.

That was his cue to shout just wait until they connected Joey Antoine to this mess and found out I used to sleep with him!

That was the lowest blow he'd ever struck at me, and it brought me up short. I did a doubletake, and saw that he was not only frustrated and upset about the newspapers and everything else that was coming at us, but seething with jealousy at the idea of Joey and me together. And it suddenly occurred to me that I had never thought to mention to him the fact that Joey and I, as I had told Charlotte, *never!*

Turning his back, he stared out the French doors that opened onto the balcony. In the distance, beyond the green levee, the river glimmered on, undisturbed.

I walked over and touched his rigid arm. "Dan, I'm going to tell you something I would have told you a long time ago, but frankly, you didn't seem like the kind of guy who would think it mattered."

Then I explained that before he entered my life, I had only experienced two less than thrilling "involvements," and Joey Antoine was not one of them.

Dan faced me, looking ashamed, and took me into his arms.

By the time Sergeant Savoy and her policewoman steno

arrived, we were reasonably calm, and making do as best we could with a pot of strong black tea.

Savoy, tired and depressed-looking, accepted tea, which was either a good sign, or she was so in need of caffeine, she wasn't particular about the company. It was only later that I discovered she had been obliged to attend Joey Antoine's autopsy just a couple of hours before.

Her uniformed stenographer, uncomfortable with the nonofficial atmosphere, declined the offer of hospitality, and focused on setting up her court reporter-type machine. The officer was tense, skinny, and bespectacled, and bore a distracting resemblance to Iola Boylan of *Mama's Family*.

Dan had to get to work, so he gave his statement first, while I waited in the kitchen. About twenty minutes later, he found me there, standing with the freezer door open, eating tangerine sherbet from the carton. I'd already polished off the leftover lemon.

"I have to go now, Claire," he said. He took my shoulders and squeezed. "God, I hate all this!" he said bitterly.

Giving an official statement wasn't nearly as much of an ordeal as I'd anticipated. The steno sat in one corner like a lump, tapping away on her machine, staring disapprovingly at the small Guido Renzi oil of an adorable angel.

Savoy had nothing different to ask, and I had nothing new to add, so it went pretty fast. Afterward, when the stenographer had packed her gear and eagerly clattered down the stairs, I broached the subject of Joey.

Nectarine Savoy's jewel-blue eyes filled with pain, and she shook her head. "Poor guy," she murmured.

"Do you think Joey's murder could be connected somehow to Angie's death?" I probed cautiously.

Savoy shrugged. "Right now, it's a tossup. Getting warned off a case he had a private stake in wouldn't stop him if he thought he was onto a lead, even if he knew he'd have to cough it up to me eventually. We've been going over his current case files, and none of them have any obvious connection with the warehouse district. Of course, he could've been going to meet a snitch. We're checking on that too."

She closed her briefcase and prepared to leave. "As it stands now, we've got no motive, and no witnesses, unless you want to count those winos who claim they saw him get out of a limousine and try to break into a building. Yeah, right!

"His wallet was still on him, and some cash, so it was either not a random mugging, or the perp got scared off, or—when they found his gun, they didn't bother with anything else."

That was comforting news! Somebody, possibly someone we knew very well, was homicidal, and now equipped with a 9mm semiautomatic Beretta.

Savoy reached the doorway and spoke again. "Joey Antoine was absolutely impossible, but he didn't deserve that. I'm going to find out who killed him."

She told me that Dan's and my statements would be ready to sign tomorrow morning, and that we should come down to Second District Headquarters on Magazine Street about nine o'clock.

It was nearly noon when Savoy left. Renee wouldn't be in until two, so it was a good time to get some exercise. I changed into bicycle pants and crop top, dragged my hair back into a ponytail under a baseball cap, and walked the half mile or so to Audubon Park. I jogged and speed-walked around for a while, then decided, as long as I was there, to visit the zoo.

First, though, I bought a large Coke and drank it at a picnic table in the shade of an ancient oak tree, while being scolded indignantly by the squirrels who reserved "their" tables for people with food.

There is something tranquilizing about strolling among your fellow creatures, who seem almost to exist in a parallel universe. I was gently nuzzled by an inquisitive giraffe, also demanding food, and exchanged a long, intent gaze with the orangutan who'd been there as long as I could remember. I always had the feeling he was trying to tell me something that I wasn't at all sure I wanted to know.

Several animals roamed freely over an area close to the river, among them an obese white Brahmin cow, who'd apparently been treated for a skin condition, her pale hide swabbed with patches of purple. A llama, who was curled elegantly on the grass, sneered down her aristocratic nose and spat, as the poor thing lumbered heavily by. "If this is karma," she seemed to be saying, "you can have it!"

I finished up, as always, standing on the bridge watching the seals cavort, so absorbed in their glorious abandonment that I started, and nearly fell into the water when my name was spoken.

It was Wilding Keller, carrying a tennis racquet and dressed in dazzling whites. My reflection bounced back at me in duplicate from the dark, Jacqueline Onassis–style sunglasses she affected.

"Oh, hey, Wilding!" I greeted her casually, wondering what on earth you say to somebody whose husband's mistress has been murdered. Especially when that same husband was about to be fired by your own ex-husband. Let Hallmark come up with a card for *that*.

"I waved at you from the tennis court, Claire," Wilding said, "but you didn't see me."

I drew a breath. "Wilding. I'm sure you know that Angie was murdered in my shop Saturday night."

Wilding leaned her elbow on the bridge and stared at the water. "Mmmm," she concurred. "It must've been awful for you, Claire. One way or another, that bitch managed to ruin everything, didn't she?"

There didn't seem to be any response to that. I was searching for a way to introduce Eustis into the conversation when she did it for me.

"I didn't hear about it until last night. I was visiting some friends in Natchez from Friday on. We were . . . skeet shooting."

"Oh, so you and Eustis were out of town until Monday night? That explains why Dan couldn't get in touch with him!"

Wilding turned her opaque gaze on me. "But Eustis didn't go to Natchez with me, Claire," she said simply. "In fact, I haven't even seen him since I got back."

I absorbed the full implications of her statement. So, it could have been Eustis who killed Angie. It could have been Eustis who'd attacked me! But why? Even if he had been Angie's love slave, I couldn't imagine him killing her because she was having an affair with Marcel. Anyway, that didn't explain Joey Antoine's death. I wasn't sure Eustis and he had even met.

And speaking of Marcel, the day Marcel Barrineau lost his silver head and killed a woman in a fit of jealous rage was the day pigs grew wings. No, there had to be somebody else involved we weren't aware of, some other reason.

Wilding was serenely oblivious that I'd been entertaining the notion of her husband as a killer. She wanted to know more about the murder, and seemed disappointed when I glossed over the gruesome details. I found her attitude rather cold, even allowing for the fact she had hated the dead woman's guts. Now, if Wilding hadn't been in Natchez . . . no, it was ridiculous!

The heat was starting to get to me, and my head began to pound at the spot where I'd been injured. I shouldn't have done all that exercise so soon.

Wilding asked if I was okay, so I told her about my own mysterious attacker.

"Poor Claire!" she remarked sympathetically. "You have had quite a time, haven't you?"

"Haven't we all?" I retorted, and told her about Charlotte Dalton's terrible experience at finding the murder story she'd been sent to cover featured her ex-lover as victim.

"Oh . . . the one who . . . arrested Dan on the news. I remember . . . seeing them . . . together . . . your party . . ."

Wilding was fading fast. I checked my watch. A quarter to two. Just enough time to get back before Renee arrived.

But Wilding had made a brief U-turn in midair. ". . . awful . . . how . . . where?"

"Oh, I don't know," I said, a little impatiently. "Some warehouse down by the waterfront. On Tchoupitoulous, I think."

The black glasses flashed. "Ahh! You mean . . . on the wharf . . . where the rats play . . ."

And then, with a flip of white tennis skirt, Wilding was gone. Her long, tanned legs carried her effortlessly across the park toward her house.

When she was some distance off, without turning around, she raised her racquet in a belated farewell, leaving me with the disturbing feeling I'd missed something very important. I had.

C h a p t e r

23

Since I had been slouching around the house for days now, I treated my command appearance at 4317 Magazine Street, home of the Second District, NOPD, as a dressup occasion.

Dan, who hadn't slept well, got up early to shower and shave, so I had the bathroom all to myself. When I entered the living room, Renee was already at work downstairs, and Dan was having coffee and orange juice, reading the morning paper. Blessedly, it carried no sequel to its article of the previous day.

He looked up as I came in, awarding an approving nod to the soft aqua gabardine suit I was wearing, with its long, low-cut jacket that fit close to the waist and followed the line of my hips, and skirt which managed to be at once both decorous and short.

For my part, I was savoring the sight of Dan in his fresh tan cotton shirt, beige linen tie with the thinnest of pink stripes, and pleated brown-and-white seersucker pants. There is seersucker, and then there is *seersucker*. The jacket lay on a side table next to his natural leather briefcase.

Dan lowered the paper and crooked a finger at me, and I went over to sit on his knee for some coffee-ish kisses.

"Do you think this jacket's too plunging for a police station?" I asked, a little gunshy after yesterday's blowup over the photograph. But today, his opinion was that it was cut exactly right for his hand to slip inside, and he proceeded to demonstrate his point.

"Hey, we better get going before they send a squad car after us," Dan said considerably later.

On the short distance to the station, I began to sense there was something Dan wasn't telling me, which meant that it wasn't totally pleasant. I didn't press, figuring I'd find out soon enough.

Amid the clamor and frenzy of crime, Sergeant Savoy ushered us into her sterile cubicle like a gracious hostess, handed us our sworn statements to read over, and alternated her attention between a mountain of paperwork and an insistent telephone.

After Dan and I signed our names, Savoy startled us by inquiring what we wanted to do with Angie's body, as it was ready to be released, and they had received a report from the French authorities that she had no living relations.

Dan gave a little cough of surprise and asked, "Uh, well. What are the options?"

Savoy ticked them off on long fingers. One, the city would handle it, with or without our financial contribution. Two, we could provide something more personal, and they would notify whatever funeral home we designated to pick her up. Three, cremation was always expedient in cases like this.

"No, positively not cremation," I said, but not because I'm opposed to the idea, per se. "Angie was a Catholic. We couldn't just violate something so basic to that."

The ball was in Dan's court. He shrugged. "We could arrange for a funeral home, even a priest," he allowed. "But when it comes to burial, there's not an extra inch of space in our family vault for anybody but my parents, and"—he darted an uncomfortable look at me—"us. Not that I'd permit it, in any event."

In New Orleans, the cemetery situation is critical. Bodies cannot be guaranteed to remain buried, because the city is beneath sea level. Instead, our choice tombs are aboveground, which over the years has inspired architecture from baroque to bizarre. Bitter battles have been waged over entombment privileges, scandals have occurred when people have literally turned up where they had no right to be, and marriages are alleged to have been contracted on the basis of either husband or wife's ability to provide a permanent roof over the other's head.

Around here, folks have always tended to be every bit as concerned about where they'll wait until that last jazz trumpet blows, as about where they'll go afterward. If not more.

Thanks to Dan, I, and any little angels we might produce, would have confirmed reservations.

Regarding Angie, however, we had come to an impasse, until I remembered Marcel's Covington property, which was equipped with a small cemetery for some of the more distant Barrineau connections. Let him help out with this!

Nectarine Savoy, at my suggestion, placed the call to Marcel herself, and as I predicted, was immediately put through to him. She explained the situation, and he agreed to the proposition at once. Just have the funeral home notify him, and he'd make the arrangements.

Savoy thanked him and was about to hang up, but apparently Marcel was still talking. "That's very kind of you, Mr. Barrineau," she replied, "but under the present circumstances, I couldn't accept. I'm sure you understand."

She listened again and frowned suddenly. "Mr. Barrineau, I'm very sorry, but Sergeant Antoine won't be keeping that appointment today. He—he was murdered Monday night."

From where we sat, we could hear the phone squawk in

astonishment. Savoy held the receiver slightly away from her ear, nodding at whatever Marcel was saying. "Yes, I know," she agreed. "It didn't get much news coverage. All right, certainly, Mr. Barrineau. I'll arrange that."

She hung up and made a note on her desk calendar. "Naturally it didn't make big headlines," she muttered. "What's the big deal? So another cop bites the dust, and in a place where he had no business to be, far as we know.

"But"—She tossed her pen aside—"on the other hand, lack of publicity gives us some room to maneuver."

"Marcel offered to do your hair too?" I inquired, and Savoy's eyes briefly glinted with amusement.

"Yes," she admitted. "And, I have to say, I was tempted. Maybe when this is all cleared up. He was trying to persuade me to come along with Joey on his appointment this afternoon."

She shook her head, marveling. "I just can't imagine Joey doing that! And Mr. Barrineau seemed very taken with him. He specifically asked to be notified about his funeral. He's not . . . ?" She drooped her wrist, and I laughed.

"Perish the thought! And of course, we all know Joey wasn't!"

Dan aimed a cross look at me, then asked, "What are the plans for . . . Joey, Sergeant?"

At least, there would be no pauper's storage shed for Sergeant Antoine. He was getting the works, a high mass in St. Louis Cathedral, and a spot in the police cemetery. There was even one faction trying to whip up support for a jazz procession through the Quarter, but they were in the minority.

"I'm waiting to hear for sure," Savoy concluded. "But it

looks like ten o'clock mass on Thursday morning, if you'd care to attend."

"Of course." I accepted the invitation, knowing Charlotte would be bound and determined to see that ordeal through, knowing she would need us.

As if my thought had conjured her up, Charlotte Dalton walked in. "There you are!" she exclaimed. "Claire, why didn't you *tell* me somebody attacked you?" she demanded indignantly.

"Between then and the time I saw you, *chér*, something much worse had happened," I reminded her gently.

Charlotte paled. "Oh, right," she murmured. "Well, did they find out who did it?"

"Ask a cop," I advised, gesturing toward Savoy, who responded with a sour little smile.

"How are you holding up, kiddo?" Dan asked Charlotte solicitously.

She sighed. "Still kind of shaky, but coming along. Thank you, guys, for being there the other night. I felt like I was going totally berserk." Charlotte straightened her shoulders. "But now, it's time to do something productive. At least one member of the press will be working very closely with the police to track down Joey's killer."

It turned out that Savoy and Charlotte were on their way to go through Joey's French Quarter apartment on Decatur Street together, hoping that this routine procedure would shed some light on what might have led him to his midnight death on the waterfront. The two women's theory was that by pooling their individual perceptions of Joey, related to what they might find there, they could make some headway not possible through the usual approaches, which were also being implemented.

"As my grandma always said, 'If you run up against a blank wall, just paint yourself a door!' " Charlotte quoted.

Gradually I became aware that Dan was shifting restlessly, sneaking peeks at his watch. It wasn't like him to let his manners slip. At least, not in public.

The four of us went down in the elevator together, and Charlotte and Nectarine got out at the lobby. They were taking Charlotte's Mercedes, which was parked around the corner. Dan wouldn't meet my eyes as we continued on to the garage. I could feel a growing tension in the air, but he didn't speak until he'd pulled out onto Magazine.

"Uh, Claire, honey," he began hesitantly, gaze fixed resolutely on the neurotic lunchtime traffic. "I've got a plane to catch. You'll have to drive the car back."

I turned to look at him. "You found it, didn't you Dan?" It wasn't really a question.

His strong hands tightened on the leather steering wheel. "Yes," he admitted.

"And, whatever *it* might be, you're taking *it* to France, right?"

Dan nodded. "Listen to me, Claire," he instructed grimly. "You are to tell nobody, underline, *nobody* where I've gone, or even that I've left town. Not my parents, not Charlotte, not anybody from the office, not the police. No matter who, or why. Promise!"

I smiled. "Why not? I'm already up to my neck in alligators with you, Dan Louis. A few more won't matter!"

He laughed. "God! I love you, woman!" Then he said seriously, "You be extra careful, darlin'. Keep the doors locked at all times. Hell, keep the car doors locked when you're driving!"

"Do you think I'm in danger, Dan?" I asked quietly, and he looked over at me, his blue eyes uncertain.

"I honestly don't know, baby. Better play it safe as possible. Believe me, if I didn't have to take care of this thing, I wouldn't leave you for a second. But if I were to tell the police what I suspect, it would blow the whole thing to hell, because I've got no proof. So, I've got to go to France to get the proof, and I don't think our pal Savoy would endorse a major witness leaving the country at this stage of the game, do you? That's why I didn't *burden* her with the decision."

Traffic had ground to a halt near a construction site on Airline Highway. I stroked his thigh, already sad at the prospect of not being able to just reach over and touch him whenever I wanted, even for a few days. Dan responded instantly, sliding sensuously down in the seat, and pulled my hand toward his zipper. "Oh, yeah," he said huskily. "Do that."

The rest of the drive was downright surreal, a jumble of impressions, gravel spattering beneath the car, impatiently honking horns, a man in an orange hardhat jammed onto long frizzy black hair stepping right in front of us, holding up a red sign that ordered STOP! Dan's laughter, and the taste of honey.

All too soon, we were turning into the airport. "How long?" I asked, still fairly dazed.

"As long as it takes, as short as possible," he replied, searching for a spot along the loading zone. "Probably not more than two or three days."

I got out and held Dan's briefcase while he took a suitcase from his cluttered trunk. He *had* been busy. A skycap trotted up for it, but Dan declined, saying it was carry-on. The skycap eyed the bag dubiously, but didn't argue since he'd gotten a tip anyway.

Well, maybe he would be able to get away with it since he was going first class overseas, and some of those flights provided more storage space than many apartment closets. At any rate, whatever *it* was, was in that suitcase.

Dan pulled me close, forestalling any questions. "Please trust me on this, baby. I'm not saying a word until I'm sure, and I never wanted to be wrong like I do now. I'll call you soon as I can. Meanwhile, you go into combat alert. Let me know if anything even slightly strange happens. And this is for whatever." He slid some folded bills into my pocket and stood looking down at me.

"I seriously love you, Claire," Dan said, and kissed me long and hard, while jets screamed overhead toward the ends of the earth and a couple of skycaps whistled and applauded.

When he had disappeared between the automatic doors, I got back into the car and drove off into the longest three days of my life.

Chapter

24

$\mathcal{I}$ took my time on the trip back from the airport, luxuriating in the BMW's airconditioned comfort and smooth handling, while a sultry Irma Thomas tape played. Cigars and aftershave and leather upholstery mingled with the sharp male tang that was exclusively Dan's, to create an effect I found distinctly intoxicating. I smiled, trying to imagine if that would show up on a breathalyser test. And how would they write up the charge? Probably a DWA: Driving While Aroused.

Before I went upstairs to change, Renee informed me that Mrs. Shelby (Hell's) Bell had come by to pick up her cologne order, only to first start carrying on because she'd specifically asked for eight boxes and there were only three. Then, when she had sprayed some on her wrist, she announced it wasn't the right fragrance!

The two of them had proceeded to wade through every bottle in every box. Twenty one-ounce bottles per box meant sixty bottles. Mrs. Shelby Bell had grown more agitated, insisting none of them were what she had bought from Angie. Renee, however, said that there were absolutely several bottles of every scent Angie had carried.

Renee offered to reimburse the woman a portion of her investment to demonstrate good faith ("I hope that was okay,

Claire."), but Mrs. S.B. had suddenly become evasive and said the money didn't matter.

I gave a ladylike snort. "And the Pope is really a Southern Baptist!"

Renee had her own theory about this. "I'll just betcha that mother possum never even paid Angie up front like she claimed! But stingy as she is, even she wouldn't lie to get money out of a dead woman, no!"

I wasn't so sure. First of all, I couldn't see Angie filling a big old special order like that without cash down. Each bottle had sold for five dollars, one hundred dollars per box. Hell's Bell had ordered eight boxes, eight hundred dollars. No way she wouldn't have to cough up a deposit.

Granted, she had probably been Angie's best single customer, buying watches and handbags by the armload, which she always claimed were for "gifts," but I suspected her of doing a very brisk turnaround trade. Between those two connivers, no telling what they'd gotten up to.

At any rate, I had more serious things to deal with at the moment. I went up and changed into my favorite "home alone" outfit of no bra, a Dan T-shirt, and panties, brewed a pitcher of iced tea, and sat down at my desk to make Angie's funeral arrangements.

This was something I never had to cope with before. Cousin Eugene had handled all the details for dear *Tante* Jeanette. I had a sudden longing for the precious dumpling woman who'd been the only mother I could remember. How I missed her sparkling brown eyes and mischievous wit! What would *Tante* J have made of all this?

Sighing, I consulted the note with the name of the funeral home Dan had given me, Serenity Chapel, and got their number from Information.

After an initial skirmish with some perky young thing

who was ill equipped to deal with what she euphemistically called my Special Needs, I was put on hold, plunged into a medley of selections from Available Music Packages. From *Cathedral Splendor*, a Bach organ fugue, which sounded suspiciously like the one Tony Perkins committed suicide to in *Phaedra*, segued into Judy Collins's "Send in the Clowns" *(Pop and Lite Rock)*. The beginning of what might have been a sample from *Sinatra Sings*: "That Was Life," was cut off by a Mr. Raymond, who professed to be thoroughly cognizant with the procedure I required.

When I identified myself, there was a slight pause on Mr. Raymond's end as he made the connection, and when I informed him the bill was to be forwarded to Blanchard, Smithson, Callant and Claiborne, I could clearly discern the rasp of his palms rubbing together.

In the end, I managed to restrain him, and we settled for the Basic and Tasteful Package: one large simple spray of roses and a black oak coffin, unembellished. I was tempted to tell him I wanted *Sinatra Sings Pop at the Cathedral*, but Mr. Raymond took his work too seriously to get the joke. The *Debussy Piano* was about as appropriate as possible. At least he'd been a French composer. But I balked when Mr. Raymond offered to book a priest from their rotating list of rabbis, ministers, and assorted gurus. It didn't feel right. Instead, I promised to notify him by tomorrow morning.

After hanging up, I sipped my tea and gave the matter some thought. Besides Marcel and Juanita, of course, the only Catholics who came immediately to mind were Wilding and Eustis Keller. Well, why not? The rest of us were paying dearly for the repercussions of Eustis getting Angie a green card. Let him at least provide the priest. It was both ironic and poetic.

I wasn't expecting Eustis himself to answer the telephone. Under the circumstances, I would have preferred dealing with Wilding, but then again, was I really up to another journey through space? Eustis, while despicable, at least operated on ground level, if not basement.

"Well, Claire!" His speech was more than a little slurred. "Is this a condolence call? 'Cause don't bother. Bitch got what was comin' to her."

"I'm not convinced anybody's got *that* coming to them, Eustis. And I certainly didn't deserve for it to come to her in my shop."

Eustis made a noise that fell somewhere between a yawn and a burp, and said nothing, so I just stated the situation baldly, not trying to spare his feelings.

He began to chuckle. "Old Danbo and Froggy picking up the tab? Oh, that's good!" he wheezed. "That's very good!"

"If you could bottle up your mirth long enough to give me the name of your parish priest, I won't take up any more of your time, Eustis," I said icily.

The word "priest" apparently stirred some primal Catholic thing deep within Eustis, because he seemed to instantly grow more sober. After hemming and hawing, he finally divulged the name of a Father Aloysious at St. Magdalena's, and agreed to pay the honorium. "In fact," he offered, surprisingly, "I'll call him myself. When is the . . . the service?"

I told him 3:00 P.M. on Friday at Serenity Chapel, and he promised to take care of it. But Eustis wasn't ready to let me go just yet. He began to barrage me with questions about the murder, such as what had the police asked us, and so on. He seemed very offended that they had dared question him and Wilding, and searched the guest house on top of that, all of which he tended to blame on Dan, not entirely convinced when I informed him he was wrong. I didn't disclose that Marcel had been the one to squeal on him.

Until now, I hadn't heard that Angie's place had been tossed before the police got to it. Although I knew Marcel had indeed been there looking for something, he wasn't the type to rip rooms apart with his bare hands.

My place had also been searched, I told Eustis. Obviously, Angie had something somebody wanted very badly? But he was not to be drawn out.

After finishing off the tea, I rinsed out the pitcher in the kitchen and poked around in the fridge to see if there was anything I could eat for dinner.

When Renee left, I carried my phone out to the pool, planning to just stretch out in a chaise and stare at the water until I fell asleep. Kevin had shown up this morning after Dan and I left, in a terrible state because his key no longer fit the lock to the garden door. The poor guy thought he was having a flashback or something. He had calmed down enough to clean the pool after Renee gave him his new key, and it sparkled seductively at me now.

One advantage of being surrounded by an eight-foot, glass-topped wall is that you can swim *au naturel*. I slipped out of my panties and T-shirt, twisted my hair in a knot to avoid the chlorine, and stepped into the water. I did a few serious laps, then paddled lazily, thinking about nothing until the phone rang. I lay back on the grey terry-covered lounge chair as I answered.

It was Charlotte, who seemed uncharacteristically at loose ends. She wanted to know if Dan would mind if the two of us had dinner tonight.

"Of course not," I assured her. "And anyway, he's going to be, ah, working late." It was true.

"Great! Chinese okay?"

We arranged to meet in our favorite Szechuan place on Conti Street in the French Quarter at about seven o'clock.

Since it was nearly six already, I ran upstairs to take a quick shower, then did my hair in a braid to keep it off my neck. I sprayed and lotioned myself with Ivoire de Balmain, and selected a sleeveless black linen dress that swirled down to midcalf, mint green quilted leather flats, and small matching shoulder bag. The emerald studs were perfect with the outfit.

I opted for a taxi, not feeling equal to the ordeal of parking in the French Quarter. Since it was still ten minutes before seven, I had the driver let me out at Canal and Royal.

Royal Street, one of my favorites in the Quarter, is crowded with antique shops and hot new boutiques, and I enjoyed looking in the windows. I was almost to Conti when something in a lighted antique jewelry display caught my eye. It was a man's wedding band, of nearly knuckle width. The surface was engraved to give the illusion of a stack of rings. I knew the perfect finger for it. I went inside.

The owner, a gnomish old gentlemen named Mr. Sidney, was just getting ready to close, but he was kind enough to show me the turn-of-the-century Italian ring. It was even more magnificent than I thought, the years since 1905 (Mr. Sidney's best guess) having imparted a soft patina to the eighteen-karat Italian gold. And it was large, definitely Dan-size.

Dan hadn't worn a ring the first time we were married, and the subject simply hadn't arisen when we were making plans for this wedding. Mr. Sidney remained wisely silent, after inviting me to hold the object. Its surface texture and heavy weight in my palm gave it a sensual purity. A sudden clear vision of Dan's left hand, wearing this ring, decided the matter.

"How much?" I asked.

Mr. Sidney blinked once, then said, "Five hundred."

Secretly, I was thrilled. I'd expected it to be at least seven or eight. But now the problem was I didn't have any credit cards with me. In addition to a few dollars for taxi fare, I'd just stuffed the cash Dan had tucked into my pocket at the airport in my little bag when I left the house. I hadn't even counted it. Of course, I could always put a deposit on the ring and pick it up tomorrow.

Mr. Sidney discreetly occupied himself while I checked my resources. I'll bet he made more money by not saying a word than others did by trying to talk you into something. I thumbed through the cash and my eyes popped. There were four five-hundred dollar bills! "For whatever," Dan had said. Well, this was it.

Casually, I inquired if there was a discount for cash, and Mr. Sidney said, in some cases, he waived the sales tax.

I wondered aloud if, in some cases, he ever threw in a little engraving.

Mr. Sidney replied that all depended.

I laid the bill on the counter in front of him and he blinked again. "What did you have in mind, Miss?"

He slid a sheet of paper to me, and I wrote something and slid it back. After reading it, Mr. Sidney gave a high-pitched giggle. "Oh, my!" He darted a sly look at me as he wrote up my receipt, brows drawing together as he tried to remember where he'd heard that name, and promised it would be ready on Monday.

It was seven-thirty when I reached the restaurant, and Charlotte was watching hungrily as the waiter prepared mu-shu chicken.

"Where have you been?" she whined. "I haven't been able to eat for days, and now that I'm starving, I've got to wait for you!"

"You *didn't* wait," I retorted, indicating her used plate, smeared with the remains of assorted *dim sum*.

"That's beside the point!" She tossed down a tiny goblet of *maotai,* which can best be described as potent rice cognac. "*Gambe!*" she laughed, pouring me a thimbleful.

The clear liquid went through my body like a cleansing fire. I'd been smarter not to drive than I'd realized, if this was going to turn into a impromptu wake for Joey.

We ordered lichee duck and kung pao shrimp, then tucked into the mu-shu pancakes. "Well," I began archly, "I have a very good reason for being late, Charlo. You see, I stopped off to buy a wedding ring."

Charlotte deftly extracted a chunk of chicken meat with her chopsticks. "Well, it's high time, honey, is all I can say. Am I invited, or is this going to be another 'I do, you do, so let's do it to it?'" She popped the chicken into her mouth and chewed ecstatically.

Since I'd wanted to surprise Charlotte by asking her in person, we hadn't sent her an invitation along with the others. Which, it now occurred to me, the printers had mailed out a few days before Angie was killed. It would certainly be interesting to see how recent events affected the RSVPs! Another glass of *maotai* further enhanced the pleasure I took in apprising Charlotte of her major role in the nuptials.

Her eyes sparkled with excitement. "My gosh! It sounds like Princess Di and Fergie rolled into one! But more important, what am *I* wearing?"

"Well, you have a choice between gold and rose, whatever style you want. Since it's going to be a late afternoon ceremony, Dan and the guys are going plain black tux, which means they'll be all set to boogie at the reception."

Dan at first had wanted me to go for the traditional ice-white wedding gown, in honor of my semivirginity, but I'd persuaded him that something more creamy would look better on me. He would flip when he saw me in the Belgian lace and silk confection, which featured a scooped and scalloped neckline, a long, straight skirt with a discreetly sexy tulip slit up the back, and misty veil attached to a big satin ribbon, all in ivory the shade of old piano keys.

As I described the gown, Charlotte's green eyes grew teary, a combination of rice wine, kung pao sauce, and sentiment. "You are so fortunate, Claire," she said with a blurry smile. "Mr. Dan Claiborne loves *and* respects you, I can tell!" She nodded wisely.

My tongue loosened by the *maotai,* I confided our unusual agreement to abstain.

Charlotte giggled and wagged her finger at me. "I *knew* it! I knew there was something bizarre going on. My God! An actual Wedding Night! That's about the sexiest thing I ever heard of!"

Then her face crumpled. "That's one of the many things that was wrong 'bout Joey and me. I tried to make it everything I wanted it to be, only there wasn't anything to begin with. Oh, he dug me, all right. But you wanna know something'? The s-e-x was never very good. For me, anyway. The whole thing was a mistake from start to finish, but when you've slept with your mistake, it makes it worse. Leastways, that's my personal opinion."

She filled our glasses again. "Let's drink to the return of the Wedding Night!" she declared loudly, causing all heads to swivel in our direction, recognizing her voice. Charlo grinned. "Film at eleven!" she promised, and everybody laughed.

But after dinner, the wake began in earnest. Charlo insisted we taxi over to the funeral home on Esplanade for visitation.

Rotating shifts of Joey's fellow cops, his only family other than that phantom father, had been keeping a twenty-four-hour vigil. Some were saying rosaries by his casket when we

entered the chapel. Charlotte clutched my bare arm with
steel fingers as we made our way slowly down the carpeted
aisle. A few officers nodded recognition to her, but she didn't
see them.

We looked down and wept at the sight of Sergeant Joseph Antoine's handsome olive face, peaceful at last. His long,
beautiful hands were clasped around a splendid rosary with
large beads of onyx and garnet. The Jesus figure gazed up at
us from the Cross, acknowledging the universal fellowship of
suffering.

Afterward we went to the Napoleon House for another
drink. At this hour, the atmosphere of quiet antiquity and
classical music was perfect for the occasion. In one corner, an
artist and an unwary tourist were hunched over a chess game,
while several couples sipped Pimm's Cup in the courtyard.
We selected a table just inside the door which opened onto
the sidewalk, and ordered Courvousiers.

I asked Charlotte if she and Sergeant Savoy had discovered anything of note in Joey's apartment. She drew circles on
the table with the stem of her snifter and looked evasive.

"Well, if the Nectarine found any evidence in his murder, she didn't tell me about it. But then, I didn't tell her what
I found either!"

What Charlotte had found was the journal Joey kept,
documenting his father search. Since it could scarcely have
anything to do with his death, Charlotte had been reluctant to
turn it over to Savoy.

"Oh, don't worry. I'll give it to her," she said, belliger-
ently, signaling the waiter for another round. "After I'm
through with it. I just haven't had a chance to read it yet."

We sipped our cognac in a morose silence, broken only by
the music, something Vivaldi-ish, the mutter of the chess players in the corner, and the occasional passerby. After nine or

ten o'clock in the evening, most foot traffic this deep into the Quarter was residential.

Suddenly Charlotte banged her glass down. "Got an idea!" she announced excitedly. "I'm going over to the TV station and edit an obituary for Joey from all that tape we shot. You know that lowdown producer hardly used any of it? And then, I'm going to throw me a hissyfit until he agrees to at least stick it on the local news tomorrow morning!"

She stood abruptly, her chair scraping noisily across the old black and white tiles, fired with enthusiasm.

Accompanied by bursts of Dixieland jazz, we walked over to Charlotte's station, which was just a block or so over and down, amid tap-dancing shoeshine boys and a throng of fun-seeking tourists, many of whom were illegally slurping Hurricanes from Pat O'Brien's lamp-shape glasses instead of go-cups. I left her at the entrance to WDSU and walked on, fortunate to spot a cab that had just delivered some guest to the Cornstalk Fence Hotel.

Soon I was home safe in bed, hugging the pillow that still smelled like Dan.

C h a p t e r

25

$\mathcal{T}$he sudden sunlight was dazzling when Charlotte and I came out of St. Louis Cathedral's dim, incense-filled sanctuary. We stood for a moment on the top step, clinging to each other in our little black hats and suits, the sonorous notes of Verdi's *Requiem* still echoing in our ears.

Across Chartres Street, a flock of Jackson Square pigeons rose flapping into the air as a phalanx of pallbearers in police uniform loaded Sergeant Joseph Antoine's splendid bronze coffin into a long, navy blue hearse.

Charlotte surveyed the ensuing commotion with grim satisfaction. The early morning news had run her "videobituary" on Joey, and there had been a respectable turnout of curiosity seekers in addition to as many members of the New Orleans Police Department as could make it. Combined with the usual flow of tourists that thronged into the square, the funeral director was losing his mind trying to organize the procession to the cemetery.

We were soon joined by Sergeant Nectarine Savoy and Detective Leo Wickes, who had asked Charlotte to ride with them to the graveside. I declined when they extended the invitation to include me, because I still had Angie's rites to contend with tomorrow. There was a limit to the amount of funereal activity I could take in forty-eight hours.

Marcel Barrineau, looking subdued but magnificent in a

charcoal linen suit, brightened when he saw Savoy. He offered them all a ride with him in his maroon Corniche, which was, as usual, parked in a No Parking zone, the windshield virginally free of tickets, also as usual. Marcel was the luckiest man in town when it came to eluding the eagle-eyed ticketers and tow trucks. The rest of us usually wound up with multiple citations wedged thickly under our wipers, or catching a taxi to bail our cars out of impoundment.

Nectarine stole a covert, appreciative glance at Marcel and another at his car, but declined with thanks, saying that her own vehicle had already been positioned in the funeral procession.

We all continued down the steps together, and I noticed Charlotte kept looking speculatively from the Corniche to Marcel and back again.

When the other three had departed, Marcel detained me. He ran a hand over his shining silver hair and said, "Claire, darling. My mirror tells me I am in need of your services. And my eyes inform me that you are in need of mine." He lifted a blond strand and rubbed the ends between his fingers. They rustled dryly. "Tsk, tsk," he reproached. "And a few highlights would not be amiss."

He was right, of course. "Your place or mine?" I inquired ironically. Obviously, he was up to something.

Marcel appeared to ponder. "Yours, darling," he decided. Surprise, surprise. "I think it's time I sampled the delights of this wonderful salon I helped to launch. Everything is, ah, sufficiently back in order? Good! Shall we say tomorrow morning, around nine?"

Angie's funeral was scheduled for three, so that would give us enough time.

"Incidentally," Marcel said as he turned toward his car,

"That was a rather . . . juicy picture of you and Dan!" He kissed his fingers to me and was off.

I had begun to walk up Chartres Street looking for a cab, when I heard my name called. From his artist's spot along the black iron railing surrounding Jackson Square, Ambrose Xavier was waving wildly.

"Where y'aat, doilin'?" he greeted me with a kiss. "I been meaning to call you but I been *beaucoup* busy! That was real bad what happened with that French broad, I met her that night at your party. Didn't like her. But what I wanted to tell you was because of them portraits I done for you what got in the T-P, people been calling me for business!"

I managed to sandwich in congratulations while Ambrose paused briefly for breath.

"So just for that, doilin', I'm gonna give you thirty percent discount off the next batch, provided you let me do them different. I'm seeing the old masters, like. You know, your Rembrandts, your Renoirs, your Reynolds. You know, the three R'uhs!" His crystal grey eyes gleamed with creative vision.

I laughed and told him it was fine by me, but he was already moving to reel in a tourist who had paused to admire his paintings, leaving me holding one of his new business cards.

AMBROSE XAVIER
Artist Extraordinaire
Portraits, Still Lifes, Landscapes
Classical to Modern
"Whatever you want, just AX!"

After lunch, Renee and I were overseeing the rehanging of the balloon shades in Angie's room (we were going to have to stop calling it that), trying to speed up the process since the reupholstered sofa, chairs, and windowseat cushions were due to arrive at two o'clock. We had attempted to space their respective deliveries as far apart as possible to avoid strife, but if these two jokers didn't hurry, they were going to overlap and there would be trouble.

In the middle of this, Charlotte telephoned. "Claire, you've got to come over right now!" she demanded.

I sighed. Granted, Charlotte had been through a terrible ordeal and needed me these days, but I had planned to use this time to help Renee get the nail salon back in shape.

"You don't understand, Claire." Charlotte correctly interpreted my hesitation. "I am not going through some postgraveside prostration here. I'm talking about the *murders*! Claire, I've *found* something!" she hissed.

Renee was more than willing to handle things on her own. "Don't worry, *chér!*" she assured me. "If those men start their stuff, I'll kick them in the *tu-tus* with my cowboy boots." She displayed the new red lizard footgear, the toes sharply tipped in gold metal. "You go on to Miss Dalton's. She needs her friends at a time like this."

Promising I'd be back soon as I could, I snared a cab on St. Charles Avenue to Charlotte's apartment on the tenth floor of a modern building overlooking the Mississippi.

I had always found the interior's muted palette of teal, bone, and magenta very soothing. She had a few stunning pieces of furniture by Starck and Saladino mixed in with sprawling vanilla velvet sofas and chairs. A Bauhaus television cabinet in pale green lacquer stood open, revealing a professional VCR monitor.

Charlotte was coiled like a spring. "First, I wanted to show you something I noticed when I was putting together that piece on Joey. You know, I hadn't even looked at the footage until last night? Watch this, Claire!"

She flicked her remote at the screen, and we were transported to the docks of Tchoupitoulous Street the night of Joey's murder, as Charlotte and her crew made their way through the chaos of flashing lights, screaming sirens, the jostle of onlookers. Two seedy-looking men approached her, and began to ramble on about a purple limousine and a man sneaking around looking into windows. Charlotte asked them which warehouse, and they waved vaguely toward the strobing red lights of a paramedic van.

Charlotte stopped the tape.

"That's it?" I inquired.

"Claire!" she exclaimed at my obtuseness. "A *purple* limousine. *Purple!* Who do we know with a fancy car that just might look like a big old purple limousine to a couple of guys who are more used to seeing pink elephants? A fancy car that could be described as purple?"

I stared at her. "You can't mean Marcel!"

Charlotte nodded vigorously. "It hit me today at the funeral when I saw that Corniche of his. It's too much of a coincidence."

"But why on earth would Marcel kill Joey?" I asked. "They'd only met one or twice."

Charlotte was triumphant. "I thought you'd never ask! Kindly peruse this volume." She handed me a thickish leatherbound book that had begun life as 200 or so blank pages.

I opened the cover to see this title:

SEARCH FOR MY FATHER
by
Joseph Antoine

"Read the next page aloud, Claire," Charlotte said softly.

> *You never knew*
> *the bitter seed of life you gave*
> *borne helplessly along*
> *upon your passion's wave.*
> *But for you*
> *my soul has always yearned.*
> *Now like a creature of the sea*
> *to my spawning place I must return.*

We were both crying by the time I finished. Here was a Joey Antoine he had never allowed either of us to know.

The following pages were a journal begun nearly two years before, after his mother's death. Names, dates, places he'd researched, records he had gained access to through persuasion or computer, intermingled with more poetry, or questions he planned to ask his father, if and when he found him. Sometimes, there were phrases penned in huge, despairing letters. "WHY ARE YOU HIDING FROM ME?"; "DADDY PLEASE COME TAKE ME HOME." And then, about eighteen months ago: "GETTING CLOSE!"

I glanced up at Charlotte, who was watching me with an oddly intent expression. "Keep going, Claire. I think you're about to discover the answer to one of your own questions."

It came with the next entry:

Was making usual patrol on Carrollton, when spotted cute blonde girl in HIS parking lot. Couldn't get her car started. Offered to hook up jumper cables. She not only works there, she's HIS personal assistant! Claire Jenner. Got telephone number.

"Oh, my God!" I was torn between relief and outrage. The oldest trick in the book! Scrape an acquaintance with one person to find out about another. Joey had simply applied his undercover investigative training to achieve personal results. That explained why, despite the total lack of chemistry, Joey had doggedly kept asking me out, and I had gone because he was goodlooking and I didn't have anything better to do. And all the time, he'd been pumping me for information about Marcel. He'd gotten it too, I now realized.

"He would ask me about the kind of people who got into the beauty business," I told Charlotte, "especially the men. He was sure no real man would want to work on women's hair for the rest of his life. They were all gay. Had to be. For instance, he bet my boss was a 'homo.' Naturally, I'd spring to Marcel's defense, and he'd act unconvinced, so I'd always wind up talking about Marcel's beautiful ex-wives, and his three little girls, his notorious reputation as a ladies' man."

I had to laugh. No wonder he'd been so angry when I quit work to marry Dan. He'd lost his connection to Marcel!

"Until he met me, when I was covering that awful story about the murdered thirteen-year-old hooker. He was in charge of the case, and we got to talking, and he found out you and I were best friends," Charlotte concluded sadly.

His association with Charlotte had put him back into the orbit of people with whom Marcel mingled socially. Only this time, there was a bonus. He had cared about Charlotte. That is, as much as he was capable of in his state of mind.

And all that class resentment had been real enough with Joey, but his expression of it had been totally dishonest. What he'd actually been saying was that he'd been denied his birthright, and he was mad as hell about it.

At first, the idea of Marcel Barrineau being the father of a thirtyish man like Joey seemed ludicrous. Until you looked at the numbers. Marcel admitted to fifty-two, which probably meant he was closer to fifty-five. Subtract thirty years from either, and you'd still have a rich Uptown French stud in his late teens, early twenties, out for what he could get. And as for attitude, well, it's no accident that the term *droit du seigneur* originated with the French.

"But I thought the whole point was the man's name was Antoine," I protested.

Charlotte reached over and flipped back some pages. "Look." She pointed to another sentence in big letters: "MY FATHER'S NAME IS MARCEL ANTOINE BARRINEAU!"

I skimmed the rest until the last few pages, where he mentioned seeing Marcel at Eclaire's opening night party, and the final entry:

Today I spoke to my father face to face for the very first time. Think he suspects who I am. Very handsome. Offered to cut my hair Wednesday. Said yes. HE'S DEFINITELY NOT GAY! Think he knows something about Angie's murder. Plan to tail him, just in case.

This was horrible. Joey had used his police credentials to gain access to the man whom he believed to be his father and to interfere in a murder case that wasn't his.

Based on Marcel's answers, Joey had smelled a rat somewhere, but instead of immediately turning over the information to Sergeant Savoy, as regulations demanded, he'd decided to follow Marcel on his own. Why? To protect him if he were guilty? Or to extract revenge upon both Marcel and the police department by doing a solo? Given Joey's inner turmoil, both were very real possibilities.

"But I still can't see Marcel as a two-time killer!" I objected.

"And why not him?" Charlotte demanded. "Somebody is, probably somebody we know too. What if he realized that Joey was his bastard son and was afraid he was going to send out a big old belated birth announcement?"

"No good," I said, with utter conviction. "Marcel would have *preened*. Especially about somebody as good-looking as Joey . . . was."

Charlotte chewed her thumb. "Well, then. Maybe he killed Joey in his official capacity as a cop. After all, Joey *did* say he was going to stay on Marcel's tail. And he *was* murdered that very same night."

"We still don't know he followed Marcel to the docks—" I began, but Charlotte chanted, "Purple limousine, purple limousine."

I sighed. "Okay. Let's just suppose you're right, hypothetically. That would mean Marcel also killed Angie. Why? Not for jealousy, I promise you!"

"What about money?" Charlo asked.

"Marcel loves the stuff," I admitted. "But I just don't see him murdering for it. After all, he was born wealthy and worked very hard to build a successful business."

But privately, I was thinking about my ransacked salon and Angie's tossed guest house. Could she have stolen something so valuable—or so incriminating—from Marcel that he would have done anything to get it back? Even kill?

Charlotte was going on speculatively. "So, let's say Marcel *did* go down to Tchoupitoulous—which I firmly believe— and Joey followed him. What's down there that would interest Marcel?"

I shrugged. "Nothing except Emeril's Restaurant is even remotely his scene. What else is there but crummy bars, warehouses . . . ?"

"Right!" Charlotte snapped her fingers. "Those old guys

said Joey was trying to see into one of those warehouses. We've got to find out who owns them, what's in them."

I checked my watch. I had to get back to the shop. "How do you plan to do that?" I inquired on my way to phone for a taxi.

Charlotte closed Joey's poignant journal and held it to her chest. "Simple," she retorted. "Ask a policeman. Excuse me. A policeperson."

I felt uneasy. "Charlotte, I want you to promise me something."

She looked up inquisitively. "Anything, Claire."

"Please, please! Do not show that diary to Nectarine until I have a chance to talk to Marcel."

Charlotte was alarmed. "Claire! You can't just patter up to that man like a little lamb and ask if he's the murderer!"

I was adamant. "Promise, Charlotte! I mean it, *chér!*"

"Okay, okay," she muttered reluctantly.

My head was whirling on the short ride back to Eclaire, but nothing like it was about to.

I got to the door and discovered I'd come away without my keys. But after I rang and knocked at the door, nobody came. My God! Where was Renee? Anxiously I began to call out her name as I beat the angel door knocker's metal wings against the wood, and punched the bell over and over.

"Claire? Is that you?" a small voice quavered at last.

"Renee! For God's sake, let me in!" I shouted, and the door creaked open.

I was about to really blast the girl, until I got a good look at her. Her rosy face had gone grey as ashes, and her slim body was shaking violently. She was clutching a striped Eclaire smock, which looked as if it had been wadded into a ball. The reek of mildew was so strong it carried across the several feet between us.

Silently she held the garment in front of her, allowing it to unfurl.

It was spattered with reddish brown stains.

Definitely *not* henna rinse.

$\mathcal{T}$he commercial-quality Speed Queen washer nestled next to a matching dryer behind discreet louvered doors. Detective Sergeant Nectarine Savoy watched stonily as the print man went through the probably pointless formality of dusting all surfaces. She was seething with fury, and didn't care who knew it. Savoy had not exactly covered herself with glory, so far.

Officer Leo Wickes, ordinarily the most stoical of men, quailed visibly when she flicked cold blue eyes at him.

This was a major fiasco, and, while there may have been plenty of reasons for it, there was not one possible excuse.

Wickes acknowledged that during the original investigation, one of the uniforms had, as standard procedure, opened the doors, noted a laundry room with stacks of clean towels and smocks folded on a long work surface built into one wall. But he, or she, had not opened the washing machine lid.

What better way to get rid of a bloodstained garment than to simply toss it into the washer with a little soap powder, turn a knob, and *voilá!* Our murderer possessed a coldly logical mind, and if that logic had extended to spot-treating the bloodstain and changing the hot water setting to cold, Renee might have thought she had somehow missed the smock when transferring a load to the dryer.

The last time Renee had done laundry was, of course,

Saturday evening, leaving the freshly folded towels and smocks in neat piles to be stowed in their respective armoires on Tuesday morning. Since subsequent events totally disrupted established routine, Renee hadn't even thought about laundry until this afternoon. And then, the only reason she'd opened the washing machine lid at all was because of the awful mildew smell.

"I thought a big rat had gotten in there and died for true," Renee explained.

After counting the Eclaire smocks she'd laundered last Saturday, and finding them all present and accounted for, it was clear that the one worn by the killer had come from the armoire where they were usually kept, along with plastic caps, waterproof capes that fastened around the neck, and, of course, boxes of disposable latex gloves.

Renee voiced a question that had occurred to me as well. "But why would somebody use a cotton smock when those plastic sheets would—would give much better protection?"

Wickes, grateful for the chance to redeem himself, even marginally, sprang into action. Taking a cape from its hook inside the armoire door, he fastened the Velcro tab around his neck and walked toward us. The material rustled and crackled noisily. For the slasher to have worn one of those sheets would have been tantamount to a rattlesnake announcing its intentions. Angie would have been alerted in plenty of time to escape.

Sergeant Savoy looked grim. "The smock means premeditation. The selection of a smock over the more practical plastic means *double* premeditation."

I had a sick certainty about something else it meant. The person who killed Angie had to be one of my regular clients, who had been here often enough to know exactly where everything was kept. Or—my stomach gave a lurch—somebody familiar with the beauty business, who could make a well-educated guess. Somebody like another hairdresser. Like Marcel.

Still, I didn't convey these thoughts to Sergeant Savoy. Maybe it was a suicidal notion, but I felt I owed Marcel a chance to come clean. That he was hiding something, I had no doubt.

Dan called around midnight, sounding full of energy. I hadn't realized how much I needed to hear his voice.

"Well, baby. Things are cooking over here. I'll know officially in a few hours whether I was right or not, but between you and me, I already know I am."

"Dan, can you tell me what it is now?"

He was silent a moment. "Sorry, Claire. Somehow, I just keep thinking you're better off if I don't. But I will say this. A small fortune can look mighty big if somebody's desperate enough for money. Big enough to kill for."

I didn't insist he tell me. I already had too much to think about, and was only too glad to unload on him, from Joey's funeral, to his journal naming Marcel as his father, to Angie's funeral arrangements, to Eustis promising to pay the priest, to Renee's ghastly discovery this afternoon.

Dan was horrified. "Oh, hell! It just never seems to end!" He groaned. At first, he was amazed about Marcel and Joey, but after thinking about it, said he could see the resemblance. Like me, he didn't think Marcel would have killed out of jealousy over Angie or fear of Joey's claims, despite Charlotte's Sherlockian deductions. He did caution me, though.

"Even if things over here turn out like I think, there's still a lot of gaps." He also agreed that Marcel, from his behavior, was certainly far from lily-white in this situation.

But I didn't even tell Dan about tomorrow's scheduled *tete à tete* with Marcel.

I sure appreciate how you're handling everything on your end, darlin'," he told me. "And I'm sorry as hell to have dumped Angie's funeral on you, but it couldn't be helped. Anyway, I am coming back on Friday night. I'm just not sure when yet. Soon as I find out, I'll let you know. Come pick me up, okay?"

"My pleasure," I murmured politely.

"Uh-uh, baby. If that ride coming is anything like it was going, the pleasure will be all mine!"

"Ah, well. You always did say I got you coming and going!" I reminded him.

"Claire, you've got me every which way there is to get me." His voice took on a certain roughness. "And guess what, darlin'? You got me right now. What are you gonna do about that, my fine little smartass?"

"Hmmm. Why don't I just . . . phone it in?" I suggested.

C h a p t e r

27

I was up early Friday morning. There was plenty to do before Marcel arrived at nine. Because my hair was so long and thick, he always insisted on it already being washed and conditioned.

The fact that this man, who was a definite link in our bizarre chain of events, would soon be using sharp scissors and chemicals on me caused no undue alarm. I remained convinced that Marcel was no killer. What he was remained to be seen. And I had a feeling I was going to see it.

I dressed in ancient jeans and once-blue work shirt, and went downstairs to get things set up, in more ways than one.

Marcel always mixed his own highlights, the palette of which varied according to mood, so all I had to do for him was get out a few bowls and applicator brushes.

I plugged in the hot wax machine—he usually liked me to do a tiny bit of shaping on his eyebrows—and made sure I had everything I needed to concoct the special silver-enhancing shampoo I had devised that could be emulsified only at the last minute, the formula for which he coveted, and which I jealously guarded.

I checked a few other details vital to my plan, and was ready with a fresh pot of coffee by the time Marcel signaled his presence upon the angel doorknocker.

"Claire, dearest!" he greeted me effusively as he swept

in, making a beeline for the pine table where the coffee was. Marcel poured a cup for each of us, and we chatted of nothing for a few moments. Then, so casually I knew he'd been leading up to it, he opened the buttery leather satchel that contained his personal tools, removed a familiar-looking square pink envelope, and offered it to me with a flourish.

"I hope I am the first to extend my sincere felicitations and RSVP your wedding, Claire," he said.

I laughed. "You are. And who knows? You could also be the last!" I slit the flap and read that Mr. Marcel Barrineau accepted with pleasure.

"Thank you, Marcel. It's good to know we'll have at least one friend rooting for us in the pews."

He shook his magnificent head portentously. "I predict this invitation will soon be the hottest ticket in town, Claire!"

He drained his cup and stood. "Well!" he said briskly. "Shall we get started?"

Just then the phone rang. It was an excited Charlotte. "Claire, about those warehouses we were discussing yesterday? I am so smart I can hardly stand myself! I couldn't get hold of Nectarine, so I called up this title research lawyer I used to date. Anyway, I persuaded him to help me out. And guess what?"

I glanced over at Marcel puttering around with tubes and bottles. "What?" I asked in a low voice.

Charlotte chuckled proudly. "One of them is leased by some Japanese vitamin company. That's where they store all their stuff for distribution. It's spelled out in the lease." She paused.

"So?" I was getting edgy.

"The other one is owned by a local businessman. Name of Marcel Barrineau!" Charlotte revealed triumphantly. "And then, when I finally talked to Savoy, I ever so casually mentioned I'd always wondered what on earth was in all those warehouses. And she kinda laughed and said she did too, but unfortunately, only got to find out when there was good reason to issue a search warrant for one of them."

"So then I just came right out and asked if they'd found anything relevant to Joey's murder in the one they'd searched, and she said no, they'd come up empty on both of them. Of course, they got kinda excited over the Japanese vitamins. But no, it was all green gama and ginseng and assorted powdered organ extracts, as advertised."

My curiosity got the better of me. "And the other?"

Charlotte's voice contained a shrug. "Well, at first they were all worked up about some kind of laboratory or factory they found. Thought it might be used to process cocaine and crack. But turns out, that's where Mr. Marcel manufactures those Marcelixir hair products he sells for a bundle in his salons." Charlo sounded disappointed. "And then, I guess he rents out space to some leather goods store because Savoy said there was a bunch of real great-looking handbags and wallets and things."

The pieces were beginning to fall into place so fast, my thoughts were rotating like a Rubik's Cube. It wouldn't take Charlotte long to add leather bags to Angie and come up with Marcel.

She was going on. "I still say, Claire, Marcel's tied up in this. And I'm going to prove it! It's too much of a coincidence!"

I happened to catch Marcel's eye at that moment. He had finished mixing his potions and was waiting impatiently for me to get off the phone. It was unfortunate that he chose to draw his forefinger across his throat in the universal gesture to "cut it short."

"You're awful quiet, Claire," Charlo complained, as if I could have gotten a word in edgewise.

"Well," I offered lamely. "You know, what with the service this afternoon and all—"

"Oh, Lord, that's right!" Charlotte exclaimed. "Don't worry, kid. I'll see you at the funeral."

Marcel was wheeling a portable steel table over to the work station. It was time to spring my little trap.

"Marcel, why don't you get into a smock and gloves while I run to the laundry room? Won't take me a minute."

I scurried out, not giving him a chance to reply. Once through the kitchen's swinging door, I slowed down, making sure to bang some pots and a few cabinets before I edged out again.

Sure enough. Marcel was prowling stealthily through Angie's room.

"Whatever it was, it's not there now, Marcel," I informed him.

He gave me a swift, calculating glance. "So you know," he remarked quietly.

My heart pounded. "Maybe you're giving me too much credit, Marcel. Why don't you tell me what I'm supposed to know."

He moved closer, and I forced myself to stand absolutely still. "About the phony designer stuff, of course!" Marcel exclaimed impatiently. "For years it has been a very lucrative racket for me, Claire. All I had to do was get a few of my operators to tell their clients about it, like they were doing this as a moonlighting thing.

"It worked like a charm! High quality goods, nothing illegal. That is, if you don't count the little matter of an enormous untaxed income, and the buyers didn't have a clue I was involved. I split everything fifty-fifty with the employee."

I let out my breath in relief as we walked back into the salon together. He was still hiding something, though. Time for the next test.

"Oh, Marcel! You better put a smock on or you'll ruin those terrific black cashmere sweats."

He looked around. "And where do you hide them, Claire? As you know, in my salons we keep them in the dressing rooms. Since you have only the one powder room, I immediately checked there, but not a smock in sight."

Touché. "Oh, I'm sorry, Marcel. In the armoire, of course." I busied myself laying out his combs and scissors as I'd done a million times before.

"Which armoire would that be?" Marcel was getting testy. "You have four of them. Lovely idea, of course. But you know, not even my famous X-ray eyes can penetrate that heavy old wood, Claire!" He leered at me exaggeratedly, and I had to laugh. If the gentleman was acting, he was way too good for me, and I might as well concede defeat. If not, then there was no problem anyway.

When I opened the correct armoire, Marcel seemed very impressed with the arrangement, voicing approval for the full-cut, heavy cotton smocks.

I sat in the chair and let him fasten one of the plastic capes around my neck. Then the artist went to work. "I am thinking, Claire, instead of ash this time, some gold streaks two shades darker than your own, plus a few reddish gold lights. Like the hair of a Raphaelite angel. And for this, I think we will give you a very wispy fringe across the brow, and along each side of the face."

He didn't ask my opinion, and I didn't bother to give one. I was in the mood for a change, and I knew instinctively that this would look terrific.

Marcel picked up his scissors, the small, extremely sharp

pair. "It is always a mistake to cut a fringe or contour the front after a highlighting is done," he lectured. "Especially if there is to be a change in style. We have all seen cases of an excellent cut, given after an excellent color procedure, with disastrous results."

I gritted my teeth as he brought the scissors close to my eyes. I mean, after all. When he began to carefully clip what seemed like one hair at a time, I relaxed.

"Sit up straight, Claire!" he barked. "Both feet in front of you, as you know!"

I obeyed meekly, and he said, very matter-of-factly, "Perhaps you will now tell me why you suspect me of murdering my lover."

Before I could catch my breath he went on. "I can supply you with several motives for myself." Snip, snip. "She was of the gutter, she was greedy, she was a cheat, she was amoral, she was a liar, and she stole from me." Snip, snip, snip. He stood behind me and tilted my head in the mirror to gauge the results, then continued his snippet-interspersed monologue.

"Of course, all that was clear to me from the beginning. But, she could also be a wickedly funny and very exciting woman, the eternal *gamine* slut. For a time, she was amusing. Then the situation grew extremely unamusing. Surprisingly, I found myself wanting something more from Angie. I was saddened to discover that she had absolutely nothing to give. I was making plans to end what had become a very complicated and unexpectedly painful entanglement. But I assure you, Claire, I did not do it by applying a razor to the throat I had kissed."

Impulsively I pulled his head down and kissed his cheek. "Dear Marcel. I never thought you did. But there are a few things I don't understand."

Marcel slipped on a pair of latex gloves and squished a

stiff brush into the bowl filled with gelatinous purple. "Do not hesitate to ask, then," he invited, applying the stuff to my hair in careful strokes.

"Well, for one thing. Dan said whoever was reproducing those designs was sailing very close to the wind. How did you manage to figure exactly how much you could get by with?"

Marcel chuckled. "It will do no harm to tell, since I am going out of that particular business. But you are so smart, Claire. And yet you cannot see the answer? Who else but Eustis?"

I gasped. Of course! It was so obvious that it wasn't! Marcel said that Eustis was always short of money and had jumped at his chance to beat the system. Eustis had also duplicated all the perfumes.

"He felt Dan had hindered him at every turn. This was his secret way of getting back at him," Marcel revealed.

"Not true," I retorted, without elaboration.

Marcel lifted a shoulder. "So I suspected. But when one is, as you say, sailing so close to the wind, one cannot be too choosy about one's legal advisor and chemist."

Marcel started the timer and sat down on a stool facing me. "What else?"

I forced myself to look straight at him. "Then there's the small matter of Joey Antoine."

Marcel actually blushed. "I had always wondered what became of the boy, but was too cowardly to find out. In any case, Adrianna did not wish it. She was very beautiful, a waitress in an Italian restaurant not far from here. Youthful lust. Youthful ignorance. I was willing to be noble, do the right thing, marry her. But my father, who was an absolute tyrant, flatly forbade such a course. He carried on so terribly, Adrianna was too frightened to oppose him.

"In the end, I managed to insist that my father settle a

substantial sum upon her. She requested that I make no attempt to see the child. And that was that. Until I started noticing a certain young man picking you up from work."

The timer *ping*ed and he rubbed a strand of my hair with a towel to check the color, deciding it needed another five minutes.

"And then, for months, nothing. You married Dan, you divorced Dan, you . . . whatever it was you have been doing with Dan. And then, I see him right here, on Eclaire's opening night. After that, fairly often around town with the charming Charlotte."

He shook his handsome head. "And then, after Angie, he turned up on my doorstep. We both knew, but nothing was said. I had planned, on Wednesday . . . but then, he was dead."

"Marcel," I said quietly. "You knew Joey was killed when he followed you to the warehouse."

Marcel looked at me and his eyes were full of pain. "I know. But I had only stopped by a few minutes to . . . check on something in my . . . little factory. It is terrible to think he . . . my son was lying dead, just a few feet away when I left. I swear to you, Claire, it makes no sense to me."

I believed him. But there was still something he wasn't telling.

For the next hour, Marcel dabbed at my hair as if it were the ceiling of the Sistine Chapel. Finally, I was looking in the mirror at a very different Claire Claiborne. Marcel's cut had left my hair still luxuriously long below the shoulders, while the fringe and wisps in front added a tousled but ladylike voluptuousness. When I moved my head, the new highlights shimmered like trapped sunbeams.

I was thrilled, and Marcel was immensely gratified by my reaction. "Dan will love it," he stated positively.

"And now, my dear!" I bowed him toward the shampoo bowl, where, as usual, he twisted his head to get a peek at my formula. While I waxed his eyebrows, we gossiped about everybody we could think of, and I decided to surprise Marcel with his own new look. Close to the sides of the head, with a slight fullness in front, and a longer back. It was very energizing, and took nearly ten years off his already youthful face.

"Claire, this is wonderful!" he exclaimed, and we discussed how long he might want to let it grow in the back.

"Nectarine will adore this," I assured him slyly, and he grinned.

"Ah, the fabulous Pomegranate! How I would love to get my hands into those beautiful copper-gold ringlets."

I was very happy to be able to report she had confessed to being tempted. Marcel was looking visionary. "I can see her almost as a Medusa."

"I'd be careful about that if I were you," I advised, brushing him down. "Wasn't she the one who turned men into stone?"

Marcel twinkled. "An event I anticipate with pleasure. Provided, of course, it is confined to the proper area."

On that incongruous note of hilarity, we parted to prepare for Angie's funeral.

But while I was cleaning the bowls where we had mixed our little secret formulas, I suddenly knew what Angie had stolen, that so many people were still looking for.

Chapter
28

*A*mong the piped-in Debussy piano selections was "Dances Sacred and Profane," and I couldn't imagine anything more appropriate for the funeral of Catherine Angelyne Labiche.

The sacred part was capably provided by Father Aloysious of St. Magdalena's, a stout fellow with bristly grey hair and big, moist blue eyes in a red Irish face. Without Father Aloysious and the comforting words from the Scriptures spoken over Angie's casket, I'm afraid the service would have taken on the macabre aspect of the old joke about the rabbi who refused to conclude the ceremony for a thoroughly unpleasant man until somebody said something good about him. It had taken quite a while but finally somebody stood up and said, "His brudder vas vorse!"

I surreptitiously polled Serenity Chapel's sparsely filled pews. Who among us could have found something good to say about Angie?

At least I could have testified that she gave excellent nail treatments. But she had also relentlessly pursued Dan.

Renee Vermilion, a black lace kerchief over her curls, sat with bowed head next to the hulking figure of Beaudine Guidry. Angie had treated Renee like an inferior servant and made an explicit move on her boyfriend; serene in crisp navy linen and straw hat, Wilding Keller had been publicly humiliated by her husband's infatuation with Angie, to the extent that the woman actually lived on her property; Eustis Keller himself, unusually pale and sober in pinstripes that looked way too hot for July, she'd seduced, used, and thrown over; Marcel Barrineau, fresh haircut gleaming in the light from stained-glass windows, had confessed that his entanglement with Angie had gotten out of control to become complicated and painful.

Of all those present, only Charlotte Dalton had no personal bone to pick with Angie. She had just detested her on general principles.

At the rear of the chapel, Sergeant Nectarine Savoy and Detective Leo Wickes were alert for signs of a quarry they were certain was in this room.

Father Aloysious wrapped up his remarks, and we all sat quietly until the final chords of "Water Music" had faded.

Immediately four large men in black suits appeared and carried Angie's coffin through a side door.

Outside Serenity Chapel, our ragged little band of ersatz mourners milled uneasily, somewhat at a loss since there was not to be the usual sequence of funeral parlor to cemetery to somebody's house for fried chicken, deviled eggs, and Aunt Anna Mae's banana pudding.

Charlotte and I, in our little black suits that were getting quite a workout of late, stood to one side. She watched with folded arms, muttering as Marcel pitched solemn woo to Nectarine Savoy, who certainly appeared intrigued.

"Claire, you've got to let me warn Nectarine about Marcel!" she demanded.

"Don't you dare!" I hissed. "Savoy's a big girl. She can well take care of herself. Anyway, you are dead wrong about him, Charlo."

She turned to look at me. "Sez who? I'm a newshound, remember? Honey, I can smell fish a mile away."

I nodded. "But this time it's a red herring, my dear." I recounted my talk with Marcel in a few brief sentences, and Charlotte sighed.

"Not only does the newshound have a stuffy nose, she hasn't been seeing too well lately either."

When Marcel and Nectarine parted, Charlotte went over and drew him aside, speaking low and earnestly. Then she pulled Joey's journal from the black Bottega Veneta satchel that accompanied her everywhere. Marcel looked like he was going to cry when she pressed it into his hands.

Obviously, she had changed her mind about the diary being evidence against him. Of course, there was still the little matter of his being in the vicinity when Joey was killed, but I righteously decided it was not my duty to point it out.

Now, Eustis was hovering around Marcel, waiting for Charlotte to leave, and Wilding drifted in my direction. She seemed oddly tranquil despite the occasion. Or maybe even because of it. I wondered how she'd react to Eustis getting the chop at Blanchard, Smithson. Where would he go? What could he do? He certainly wouldn't be able to afford his little bits of fluff any more. A thought struck me. Wilding, holding the purse strings, would now be in complete control. She'd virtually own him. *Unless he managed to get rid of her too!*

I felt a chill as a drop of perspiration trickled down my back. I didn't know how Joey fit in, but suddenly, I was convinced that Eustis, his insecure masculinity pushed beyond endurance, had killed Angie! The scenario played itself out in my head. Eustis, searching for Angie, finding her at the shop, waiting for someone else. Who? Marcel, probably, who claimed to have been out of town.

Eustis, begging and pleading, Angie, taunting, dismissing him, turning her back to do something, ignoring him. Eustis, pretending to leave, maybe spotting the razor in the case, getting the idea. Quietly opening an armoire, wrapping himself in a smock, putting on gloves, sneaking up behind her, one cut, all over.

He had been to Eclaire often enough to have some idea where things were kept, where the laundry room was. And now that I knew what he'd been looking for, I could understand why he would go berserk enough to tear the place apart trying to find it.

Dan had said it was a small fortune, but big enough to kill for. Who else but Eustis so desperately needed his own money? And now, for the first time in their marriage, his enormously wealthy wife would have him over a barrel. He had demonstrated what he was capable of when goaded. Possibly he wouldn't even have to kill her. If Wilding wasn't so rich, she might have been considered certifiable long ago, instead of merely "eccentric." All Eustis would have to do would be to drop a few words here and there. It wouldn't take long for the rumors to start. And then a nice little sanitorium for the poor crazy wife, while the husband "oversaw" her finances.

Of course, I could prove none of this. How could I even hint such things to Wilding? In any case, I was spared the necessity for a decision because Savoy intercepted her before she reached me.

Renee and Beaudine came up. Beau was going to take her back to Eclaire, and she wanted to know if it was okay for them to have some of the wine and cheese that was in the downstairs refrigerator.

I urged them to help themselves to anything they found, and asked Renee if she would stay in the salon until I got back. Checking my watch, I saw that it was nearly four o'clock. I needed to do a little shopping first, so I told them I'd return before six.

Charlotte concluded her discussion with Marcel, and Eustis immediately pounced on him. "You were right about Marcel, Claire," Charlotte admitted when she rejoined me. "He even said he had already planned to tell Savoy the whole story. He called her 'Guava,' though."

I was relieved that Marcel had volunteered to give the information to the police himself, and I felt vindicated in my defense of him.

"I'm going back to the station now Claire," Charlotte said. "Can I drop you someplace?"

"No thanks, Charlo." I indicated the BMW in the parking lot. "I've got Dan's car today."

"Hey, that's who's missing!" Charlo exclaimed. "Where *is* Dan, anyway?"

Before I could reply, Savoy and Wickes approached. "I was about to ask you the same question, Claire," Nectarine said.

"He felt just terrible he couldn't make it," I told them, with as much conviction as I could muster. "But some emergency came up and he simply wasn't able to get away in time." It was the literal truth.

Savoy looked like she wanted to say more, but just then, the funeral attendants appeared carrying the coffin, and slid it into the back of the dark grey hearse. The uniformed driver climbed behind the wheel, and Marcel got into the front seat beside him, escorting Angie on their final journey together.

After a moment of silence, Wilding hurried Eustis toward their Mercedes wagon. Beaudine and Renee were already gone, so while Charlotte was talking to Savoy and Wickes, I unobtrusively made my way to Dan's car and was exiting the parking lot, waving a casual farewell to the remaining trio, before they even realized I was leaving.

I spent the next hour and a half looking for the perfect

dress to pick up Dan at the airport, and found it at Fancy's Finery. Strapless dull bronze silk, with a short full skirt cinched tightly at the waist by a wide black snakeskin belt. A cropped black silk jacket made it plain enough not to look too conspicuous for the airport waiting room, jazzy enough if we stopped off for dinner or drinks on the way home.

It was just gone six when I got back to Eclaire and let myself in, surprising Renee and Beaudine smooching on a sofa. Beau turned nearly as red as his curly hair, and Renee was flustered.

"Oh, Claire! We were just, uh——" she stammered.

I put my packages down by the stairs and pretended not to notice. Of course I wouldn't reprimand her, but I didn't want her to start taking liberties either. When I looked up again, Beaudine was perched stiffly on the edge of the sofa, and Renee was over at her desk.

"Hi, y'all," I said casually. "Anything I need to know about?"

Renee let out a relieved breath and we went through a stack of messages together. Then she said, "Oh, and Dan left word on the machine for you to please pick him up at eight tonight."

As the two lovebirds straggled toward the door, Renee remembered to tell me that Mrs. Keller had dropped by looking for me shortly before I arrived. That was odd. I'd just seen Wilding, and I didn't feel like getting beamed up so soon after I'd glimpsed the future Eustis might be planning for her.

"Did she leave a message?"

Renee looked vague. "Umm, no. She just asked if she could use the powder room. And then Beau accidentally broke two of your wineglasses in the kitchen."

Beaudine turned even redder. "I'm sorry, Claire," he mumbled. "I'm going to buy you a whole new set."

"—and when I came out again, Mrs. Keller was gone," Renee finished.

It was a reprieve, I thought, carrying my Fancy's Finery shopping bag upstairs. But how long could I put off telling my friend, however loony, that I thought her husband was a killer who might be intending to have her institutionalized so he could get his greedy little paws on her great big money?

I put the Keller misery out of my mind as I showered, then powdered and perfumed myself with Ivoire, Dan's favorite fragrance on me. The bronze silk seemed to swirl over my skin like coffee into cream, and set off the new lights in my hair. Fortunately, I had a pair of black snake pumps with an hourglass heel that went perfectly with the wide belt, and they were comfy enough that I didn't need to bother with pantyhose. In fact, the only lingerie I wore was a pair of peach lace panties. All the better to . . .

Putting things into a black shoulder bag, I picked up the jacket and hurried downstairs, tingling all over at the thought of seeing Dan, hooked and loving it. Small wonder then, that I was taken completely off guard when I opened the door to go out. Suddenly the knob was jerked from my hand, and I was shoved roughly back inside.

My God, it was Eustis! More drunk and dangerous than I had ever seen him before. He gripped my bare arms tightly, and I dropped my bag and jacket. His rancid breath assaulted my nostrils as he shouted at me.

"All right, bitch! Where is it? You better tell me now!" He slapped my face, hard.

"What?" I managed to gasp out. "What are you talking about, Eustis?"

He shook me like a stuffed doll. "Don't play games with me, you little coonass cunt. That's all you are, a no-good little coonass cunt!"

Eustis let go of me suddenly, and I staggered back under the row of Ambrose Xavier portraits, catching myself before falling onto the hard tile floor. My arms were a livid red from his grasp.

He stood hunched forward agressively, fists clenched. He looked frightening and pitiful, still dressed in the unseasonably warm suit he'd worn to the funeral. Now his tie was askew, and his shirt front sported a dark stain where he'd evidently spilled a drink on himself.

I tried to speak calmly. "What is it you think I've got, Eustis?"

"As if you didn't know, you slut!" He sneered. "You and Dan and Angie and Marcel planned it all. After I did all the work. *All* the work!" he shouted, and started toward me again.

I cringed into the wall, looking for something to use as a weapon, but there was nothing. I stayed still. If he killed Joey, he had a great big Beretta in his pocket, and I was taking no chances.

"That's a lie, Eustis!" I said rapidly. "Angie made her own plans, as you must know better than anyone. She would hardly include me in them."

Surprisingly, his face crumpled. "I loved her, Claire!" He sobbed. "I risked everything for her." He stood in front of me, blocking my escape, determined to pour out the whole sordid story before he did whatever he planned to do to me.

"We met in Paris and fell in love. At least, I did. She told me she wanted to come to America to be with me. Then she said Bertrand Gillaud had told her certain things he shouldn't have. For instance, Bertrand and his brother each had half of the formula for La Poire, and neither of them knew where the other was kept. But Angie knew where Bertrand's was, because the fool told her.

"I guess I wanted to show off, so I said if she could get Bertrand's half, I could experiment until I figured out the other half. She laughed and said it would be the perfect way to get even with them for firing her."

So Angie had stolen the formula, and Eustis had gotten her a green card and brought her to live practically under his wife's roof. Then he began to work day and night on La Poire at Marcel's factory, with Marcel's approval. Only this time, it was going to be a real counterfeit operation.

Marcel found someone who could duplicate the bottles and labels Gillaud used for their La Poire spray, and lined up reputable distributors who were willing to supply this "limited edition" to expensive department stores throughout the South and up the Eastern Seaboard. It is a fairly common practice for a famous maker to unload costly unsold product at a bargain price in starkly packaged "limited editions." We had had plenty of them when I was still working in the department store.

No cosmetics buyer would have been suspicious, or anything but delighted, at the prospect of getting their hands on a gross or two of La Poire spray they could sell for twenty-five bucks a bottle and still clear a huge profit. The stuff would go like hotcakes.

It might have taken a year or two for anybody to catch on. After all, nobody was likely to call up Poire Gillaud and question them. And by then Marcel, Angie, and Eustis would have raked in *beaucoup* tax-free bucks. Nothing would have been simpler than to fold their tent and become invisible when the alarm finally went out. It was a perfect scheme.

But Angie had gotten greedy. When Eustis perfected his first batch of La Poire, it had been bottled in the same manner as the frankly *faux* scents she was already selling, waiting to go out as samples for the distributors to use to hook buyers.

Angie's biggest customer, Mrs. Shelby Bell, must've said something to the effect it was too bad none of those sold by Angie smelled like La Poire, which was the only perfume she ever used.

The temptation was too much for Angie. She'd been stealing a box here and there of the stuff for Mrs. Bell, whose demands for product increased with her own turnover. And inevitably, Marcel and Eustis discovered what she was doing.

Then, unbelievably, Angie had stolen the complete formula for La Poire from Eustis!

He had confronted her the night of the murder. "And she laughed at me, Claire!" he wailed piteously. "She said if I wanted it, I could either figure it out again, or find it where she'd hidden it. She said it was right in front of my—my stupid eyes. I nearly went nuts looking for it, and she just sat there and laughed and laughed at me."

"But what could Angie have possibly done with the formula on her own?" I couldn't help asking. "After all, everything had already been set up. She had as much to lose as you did."

Eustis looked confused. "Don't try to fool me," he said, uncertainly. "You were all in it together. Cutting me out, leaving me with nothing. *Nothing!*" he yelled.

"She told you that?" I inquired, with real curiosity.

"She didn't have to!" Eustis stormed. "I knew! She could get any man to do what she wanted!"

I wasn't about to shatter his illusions by contradicting that statement. Because I had just realized what Angie had wanted, why she'd looked both exalted and terrified that night. There was only one thing Angie could have possibly thought she'd gain by stealing that formula, something Eustis would never have grasped. Marriage to the one man she loved, as much as she was capable of loving. The man she knew she was losing.

Angie had stolen the thing she thought was most valuable to him, planning to hold it over his head, perhaps even threatening to implicate him to the authorities if he didn't marry her. But as usual, her blindness to all needs but her own had caused her to misjudge and overstep.

Even her farcical pursuit of Dan had been primarily for Marcel's benefit. Dan had tolerated it because he suspected some connection with the theft at Poire Gillaud the moment I told him about her. He must've gotten Bertrand to come clean with the whole story then.

Tragically, Angie had no idea that there had been a window in time when Marcel was actually disposed to make a commitment, before he'd realized how twisted she was. Her last bid for respectability had gotten her throat cut for her.

"All my life," Eustis was saying, "always the same. Everybody gets what I'm s'posed to have. 'Specially Danbo. Danbo signs the best recruits. Danbo's got a lot of money. Danbo's a senior partner. Danbo got Angie after him. He even got you!"

His piggy little eyes fastened on my chest. "I was s'posed to get you, Claire. I had it all planned. And then Danbo took you."

He lurched forward. "Lemme see those big tits, cunt!" Eustis mashed me against the wall and tried to drag the top of my dress down, but I managed to stomp on his foot.

Suddenly the front door flew open and Eustis went sailing backward. Like an avenging angel, Dan had appeared from nowhere and immobilized Eustis, pinning both arms behind his back.

"I knew something was wrong when you weren't waiting!" Dan panted, jerking Eustis roughly. "I called the police and got a taxi and just hauled ass."

"Darling, be careful. He probably has a gun," I warned.

Eustis snapped his head up. "You must be crazy," he said thickly.

"You stole it when you killed Joey Antoine!" I accused.

"I didn't kill anybody!" Eustis quavered. "Honest!"

"I know that, Tick," Dan said soothingly. "I just haven't had a chance to tell Claire that it was—"

"I, said the fly!" came a dreamy voice I knew so well, and Wilding Keller walked in from the powder room, pointing Joey Antoine's 9mm semiautomatic Beretta.

C h a p t e r

29

"*Y*ou never went to Natchez, Wilding," Dan said. "You just left the house and waited to see where Eustis would go."

Wilding's beautiful head tilted appreciatively at Dan. "True. Unfortunately, the police also thought to check my alibi. They asked me for my friends' number at the funeral today. I had made up my mind that bitch wouldn't make Eustis suffer any more. Things were bad enough when they—well, you know. But after she dropped him, life became intolerable."

Eustis hung his drunken head, and she laughed. I could only imagine what horror their existence together must have been.

Wilding came closer, holding the gun with a steady hand, and I remembered she was a crack shot. I hardly breathed. "I followed Eustis here that night and saw him use the key in the door knocker to get in."

Dan and I exchanged looks. Some great idea that had turned out to be.

"So," Wilding continued, "I waited a few moments, then did the same. I heard the whole thing, and realized Angie was planning to blackmail Marcel into marriage."

Eustis looked amazed, and even Dan seemed surprised. Marriage was not the kind of motive that would immediately occur to a man.

"There was no chance she would ever go back to Eustis. She wasn't the least bit concerned that she was destroying him. Therefore, I decided to destroy her."

Wilding remained concealed in the powder room (as she had done tonight) until Eustis finished with his rampage. When he left, Wilding simply put on a smock and gloves from the armoire where she had seen them every week, took the razor from its case, and slipped up behind Angie.

"I'm sorry about the wall, Claire," Wilding apologized. "But then, I couldn't exactly ask her to move, could I?"

Wilding then stuck the gloves in the trash compactor and the smock in the washing machine, planning to come back and clean the wall and remove Angie's body from the house. "That way, Claire, you would think it was only a robbery," Wilding explained. "But just when I'd pulled her into the salon, I heard somebody else using the key." That "secret" key was getting to be a very unfunny joke.

So she had nipped back into the powder room and peered through a crack in the door to see Marcel enter. He had cried out when he'd discovered Angie lying there, and bent over the body for a moment. Then he had gone into Angie's room, which gave Wilding a chance to escape.

"It was too late then, Claire," she said ruefully. "I tried, I really did."

Dan was still holding Eustis, and Wilding pointed the gun at him. "Let him go, Dan!" she ordered crisply, and he obeyed.

"Wilding." Dan spoke quietly. "Why did you stab Joey?"

She shrugged. "Well, how could I know he wasn't handling the case? After all, he'd been strutting around on television." *That* was what had been bothering me about what Wilding said when I saw her in the park! There was no way she could have seen New Orleans news from Natchez, Mississippi.

Wilding said, "See, I had finally discovered what was going on down at that warehouse. Since Angie ripped off the formula, Eustis was there at all hours trying to figure it out again. He even came back here to look for it. And naturally, I followed him.

"The next night, I'm afraid I let him go ahead and hit you Claire. After all, I wanted him to find the formula before it incriminated him. He can really pack a punch, can't he?" she mused, with terrible fondness.

"When I saw Sergeant Antoine prowling around, I thought he must have found out about the theft in Paris somehow and connected Eustis. Well, I couldn't allow that. I happened to have a hunting knife in my purse. A girl can't be too careful these days, you know. I wrapped the handle in a Kleenex, and that was that."

She indicated Eustis. "I had to protect him, you see. He isn't much, but he's all I've got."

The woman was totally mad. No wonder I had always sensed the aura of decay hovering over her beautiful home. It was in the very air we were breathing right now. She raised the gun again, and Dan yanked me behind him.

Wilding looked mildly puzzled. "Oh, Dan. I'm . . . sorry. I . . . wasn't going to . . . shoot you and Claire . . . always been my . . . friend."

Her eyes sharpened as she heard the sound of sirens. "Don't follow us. Come on, Eustis."

Eustis didn't look at us as he moved in front of Wilding, but suddenly he stopped and stared at the row of Ambrose Xaviers. And he began to laugh, crazily. "Wh-what a joke!" he sputtered, pointing at the portrait of the man reading the newspaper. "She wrote the formula right on the front page!"

I looked at Dan and he nodded. Later, he told me that Angie had also concealed the packages of cologne intended for Mrs. Shelby Bell behind the paintings. When Dan spotted the formula, he'd moved the man with the newspaper slightly, and one box had fallen to the floor, leading him to examine the others.

Eustis was burbling hysterically now. "Hush, darling. Come along," Wilding crooned, and they disappeared into the kitchen. We could hear the French doors to the backyard open and close, as the sirens screamed up the driveway.

A moment later, Sergeant Savoy, Officer Wickes, and four uniformed officers burst into the room, guns drawn.

"Where?" Savoy barked, tersely just as the first shot rang out.

The police contingent charged toward the sound, but too late to prevent the second shot.

Wilding had effectively gotten rid of the Tick. She went for the head. Then she had put the gun into her mouth and blasted her own away.

The next day a flock of pink envelopes lay scattered on the floor beneath my mail slot. I picked one up at random to read:

Mr. and Mrs. Eustis P. Keller regret that they will be unable to attend . . .

C h a p t e r

30

La bonne femme quelle hot stuff
Me burn my hand on she fryin' pan
La bonne femme quelle hot stuff
She pepper make my swizzle sizzle
La bonne femme quelle hot stuff
Yeah, chér!

To uproarious laughter and applause, Dan finished his duet with Bubba Smoke, jumped down from the stage, and swept me around the dance floor of the Pontchartrain Hotel's Grand Court to the wail of fiddles and accordions and clatter of thimbled fingers on washboards.

The tulip slit up the back of my ivory lace dress made it perfect for dancing, and I followed easily as Dan dipped and twirled and caught me close, flashing his big wedding band that was inscribed "The Boss." It was heaven.

The pear-shaped diamond had been relegated to my right hand to make room for my own new wedding ring, which was Dan's surprise to me: another large canary diamond on a wide gold band, this one in the shape of a heart.

Our wedding day had been the kind of perfection most every teenage girl used to dream about, beginning with the early morning delivery of my bridal bouquet of Brandy roses—accompanied by Dan's gift, a pavé diamond heart pendant and matching dangling earrings—to the moment Dave Louis Claiborne escorted me down the aisle and handed me over to his son, to the look on Dan's face when the priest said, "You may kiss your bride."

Charlotte had spent the night with me, and we'd stayed awake talking into the wee hours. She was very excited about Foley Callant, with whom Dan had fixed her up three weeks before. Since Foley was going to be Dan's best man and Charlo my maid of honor, it just made sense for them to get acquainted ahead of time. Charlotte had protested that she didn't want to be a pity date, and Dan had retorted that pity was the last thing Foley Callant would have on his mind when he got a look at her.

It was an instant success. Foley was nearly as big as Dan and twice as rich, a strawberry blond, blue-eyed Baptist.

But they were both going slow. Foley was still smarting from Belinda dumping him for a younger man and taking off to Santa Fe to make pottery or something, and Charlo wanted to be sure she never again settled for less than she needed. Because, as she pointed out, if you do, you get what you deserve.

Now Dan whispered, "Look at Foley and Charlotte." Foley, resplendent in tuxedo, and Charlotte, in her gorgeous gold satin gown, were dancing together as if they were born to do so.

The champagne was flowing and things were getting pretty rowdy, in a nice sort of way. It was hilarious to see a roomful of New Orleans society jiggling to Cajun music and yelling out "Yeah, *chér!*"

Dan looked down at me, touching the diamond hearts at my throat and ears. "God, you look good enough to eat, and I am not ruling out that possibility, understand?"

I melted into my husband. "I was thinking you looked

pretty tasty yourself." I laughed when he pulled me tighter to him so I could feel his response to that remark. "I can't believe we finally made it," I murmured.

He said with conviction, "Oh, I can promise you, you will before this night is over. I am going to . . ." And he proceeded to inform me of his plans while we danced slow and close.

The rest of the evening passed in a blur of music and dancing, laughter, food, sentimental and bawdy toasts, video recorders, popping corks, and flashing cameras. We cut the cake, an incredibly lush, dense, lemon thing, and posed for more pictures.

A mildly inebriated Charlotte grabbed my arm. Her beautiful face was flushed, and her green eyes glittered excitedly. "Claire, Claire! I finally figured out what's been wrong with me and men all this time! See, I kept hooking up with those angry, exotic types because I was rebelling against my background, which my grandmother always claimed she expected ever since I displayed a marked preference for Acorn pattern silverware. But then, all of a sudden, I stopped and thought, hey! What's so wrong with my background? Well, I got Pure D honest and admitted that all I ever really wanted was a rowdy frat daddy, preferably Baptist, with a great big dong and lots of money who knows what to do with both of 'em!"

Foley Callant, pretty flushed himself, had come up behind her and was unabashedly eavesdropping. Now he slipped an arm around her narrow waist and informed her, "Well, darlin', I think something could be done about that."

Charlotte batted her lashes demurely. "Oh? Are you personally acquainted with a gentlemen who answers to that description, Foley?"

As they walked off together, Charlotte was asking Foley where he stood on Wedding Nights.

Then Dan and I were onstage, and he threw my garter directly to Foley. I, of course, made sure Charlotte caught the bouquet. Amid applause, rice, and Bubba Smoke saying "And awaay they go!" over a musical flourish, we sprinted laughing into the elevator that carried us to the penthouse suite, which occupies the entire twelfth floor of the Pontchartrain Hotel.

The diamond hearts winked at me conspiratorially in the mirror as I brushed out my long hair and slipped into the pink charmeuse teddy and matching ankle-length robe. On my feet were pink satin mules with extremely high heels and big bows on the toes.

Dan was already waiting for me in the living room, stretched comfortably out in a big chair with the lights of New Orleans and boats on the river twinkling behind him. The Jacuzzi bubbled merrily, and a bottle of Cristal '81 nestled in its silver bucket of ice.

When I entered, Dan put down his cigar and pulled me onto his lap. He looked wonderful in my wedding present to him, a robe of thick silver silk. At first, I thought he wasn't wearing anything underneath, but I was soon proven wrong.

He had put on the "Be Mine Valentine" briefs, and like he promised, there was no shortage in the arrow department!